COWBOYS can't LIE

BOOKS BY RACHEL BRANTON

Finding Home Series
Take Me Home
All That I Love
Then I Found You

Lily's House Series
House Without Lies
Tell Me No Lies
Your Eyes Don't Lie
Hearts Never Lie
Broken Lies
No Secrets or Lies
Cowboys Can't Lie

Noble Hearts
Royal Quest
Royal Dance

Picture Books
I Don't Want To Eat
Bugs
I Don't Want to Have
Hot Toes

UNDER THE NAME TEYLA BRANTON

Unbounded Series
The Change
The Cure
The Escape
The Reckoning
The Takeover

Unbounded Novellas
Ava's Revenge
Mortal Brother
Lethal Engagement
Set Ablaze

Imprints Series
Touch of Rain
On The Hunt
Upstaged
Under Fire
Blinded

Colony Six Series
Sketches
Visions

Other
Times Nine

COWBOYS
can't LIE

RACHEL
BRANTON

WHITE
STAR
PRESS

This is a work of fiction, and the views expressed herein are the sole responsibility of the author. Likewise, certain characters, places, and incidents are the product of the author's imagination, and any resemblance to actual persons, living or dead, or actual events or locales, is entirely coincidental.

Cowboys Can't Lie (Lily's House Book 7)

Published by White Star Press
P.O. Box 353
American Fork, Utah 84003

Printed in the United States of America
ISBN: 978-1-948982-06-1
Year of first printing: 2018

TARA'S
FALL

1

He emerged from the upscale horse barn and strode toward her with a confident swagger and a smile that had probably broken a million hearts. Her eyes riveted on the man, unable to pull away. Tara Levine had never been attracted to cowboys with those stiff boots and ridiculous hats, like fake relics from an old western, but Crew Ashman, owner of the Silver A Ranch, was different.

His worn hat sat low over his eyes, shielding them from the burning sun without hiding his compelling gaze. His strong, bronzed arms made a decided contrast with his white, oddly clean T-shirt that stretched slightly across the wide expanse of his chest. His jeans were loose enough to be comfortable but tight enough to hint at powerful legs beneath the material, and his dark cowboy boots looked as if they were an extension of his body. He appeared comfortable even under the impressive heat of the Arizona sun.

By contrast, she felt hot and sticky in her bright blue suit that had been meant to impress. She was sure the glistening sweat rolling down her face near her hairline was impressing no one, and least of all this cowboy, who was now staring at her with a challenge behind the smile.

"Good afternoon," he drawled. "My stable manager said you wanted to see me?" Up close, his tanned face was almost too perfect, but a five o'clock shadow somehow softened his face, making him more human. She could see laugh lines around his mouth and eyes that further enhanced his ruggedness. Laughter was a good sign. Maybe coming here was the right thing to do.

"Hi, I'm Tara Levine." She offered her hand. "You're Crew Ashman, right? I'd like to talk to you about your horses."

His gaze dipped to her hand, as though considering it for a moment. Finally, his hand enveloped hers, feeling deliciously cool and strong against her skin. A current of something unidentifiable rocketed up her arm, and she pulled back a little too abruptly.

His smile grew, as if he suspected how his touch affected her. "You should have called," he said. "I would have saved you the trip."

What? Tara bristled internally. She knew he might need a little convincing to give her what she wanted, but she hadn't even launched into her practiced spiel. "If you'll just give me one moment—"

"I'm sorry, but I'm not selling Iron Express." There was a hint of steel in his voice that belied his pleasant expression. "However, I'm willing to discuss breeding services, if you'd like to offer them to your clients."

"But—"

"He's not for sale." The suggestion of steel had grown into an entire wall now. "Look, I already gave your boss my answer last week. Iron Express is not for sale, and my offer to buy back Jump Start still stands. Thank you for coming." He gave a sharp nod and started to turn on his heel.

What a jerk! "I'm not here for your horses," Tara finally recovered enough to say. "I mean, I am, in a way, but not Iron Express. I have no idea what you're talking about."

He stopped, his eyes running down her face to her suit and on to the high heels that were as out of place here as his spurs would have been at the marketing firm where she worked.

"Dervin King from High Vista didn't send you?"

There was a story behind his question, Tara guessed, and she wondered if answering him would set him off again. "Well, he did recommend that I come here."

His glare should have frozen her. Instead, sweat dribbled down the back of her neck under her long hair. His jaw clenched and unclenched, and she had the feeling he was fighting to stay calm.

"But I'm not affiliated with High Vista in any way," she added in a rush.

"Oh? Then what can I do for you?" He didn't seem to believe her, but at least he was listening.

"I'm from Lily's House," she said. "It's a group foster home for teen girls in need. They usually have about ten foster children there at any given time, and sometimes more when it's needed."

"I've heard of them." His voice was more relaxed now, and weariness showed in his eyes. "You work there?"

She shook her head. "Not really. I mean, not as an employee. I just volunteer. Most of us do." She could have bitten her tongue as the last few words escaped. She meant "most of us do after we age out," but she didn't need him to know that she'd grown up at Lily's House.

"Most of us?" He quirked a brow in a way that was undeniably attractive. His eyes were a deep brown that reminded her of warm nights and laughter. The same color of the short hair that escaped from under his hat.

I do not like cowboys, she reminded herself. "I'm sorry. I meant, most of us who work there are volunteers. Lily Perez and her husband are the foster parents."

"So there actually is someone named Lily."

"Yes. She's pretty great." A rush of emotion threatened to choke Tara. Lily had saved her life, had become the one constant in a world where nothing was guaranteed.

His eyes didn't waver from her face, and they seemed to see too much. For several seconds, neither of them spoke, and then he said, "I guess she'd have to be."

He glanced behind him at the elaborate barn that looked better than some motels she'd stayed in. The colored cement corridor between the rows of stalls joined a walkway that led to a training area, where the stable hand she'd talked to earlier was working with a beautiful chestnut horse.

She waved toward the men. "I can come back, if you're busy."

"No, it's fine. Come on. Let's talk on our way up to the house."

"Okay." That was a surprise. One minute his glare was ready to freeze her to death and now he wanted to chat at the house? No. More likely, he needed to go up to the house and was hoping to get rid of her once and for all on the way. If his strides were any indication of how much time he was willing to give her, she'd better talk fast.

Well, she was no dainty little princess. She stretched to match his pace, using her arms to propel her further. "Mr. Ashman, I—" The heel of her right pump caught in a groove where two pieces of cement joined. She stumbled and might have fallen if his hand hadn't whipped out to grab her arm.

Her face burned. "Thanks." She hated how breathy she sounded, but all of a sudden her heart was beating too fast, and she was quite certain it wasn't because of her near fall.

"Sorry about that." He dropped his hand and began walking again, but more slowly this time, eyes scanning the walk ahead for more joints. "And, please, call me Crew. Now what were you saying?"

They had reached the place where the walkway either led into the parking lot or curved up to the house. Probably two minutes of talking time left, if that was all he would give her.

"The Silver A Ranch is one of most respected horse-boarding and horse-training facilities in Phoenix," she began.

He cast a lazy smile at her that started her flushing again. Hopefully, he'd attribute it all to the heat and her near fall. "There aren't really that many of us. At least if you're talking high-class Thoroughbreds."

"You mean there's you and High Vista."

His lip curled slightly and a furrow appeared between his brow. "Yes. But while horses are often what the average person thinks of when they hear about us, keep in mind that first and foremost, I raise cattle."

She hadn't known that, which told her she hadn't done enough research. But she needed to get back to the point at hand because the house was looming in front of them.

"So, Mr. Ashman—Crew—most of the girls work with Lily's sister, who is a psychologist, because they all come from neglectful or abusive situations." She paused, taking a peek at his face, which showed no expression. What was he thinking? "But they need more than just talk. So we get them involved in school, sports, music, art, and numerous others projects to help them find themselves and learn what's out there." Tara's voice increase in speed as they approached the back deck of the house. "You know, give them the opportunities that they didn't have in their own families. I think—"

"Here we are." He stopped before the deck and leaned sideways past her to open another door she'd thought led to a garage. His arm brushed hers and for a moment she was distracted by his closeness.

"After you," he said, gesturing for her to proceed him into the house. "And please continue."

The cool air hit her first, followed by the aroma of rich leather. As her eyes adjusted to the dimmer interior light, she saw an office—a very masculine office—filled with an expensive-looking desk and bookshelf. Below the large window that faced the back yard and the barn sat a worktable filled with harnesses and at least two saddles. Tara was willing to bet that was where the smell came from and not from the black chair behind the desk.

"You see, some of the girls don't react to the normal methods of getting them to talk and recover," she said as he rounded the desk and pulled open a drawer, where he removed a pen and some kind of ledger. "We've discovered that giving the girls something living to take care of often helps reach them in ways nothing else does."

She stopped talking, her chest suddenly tight. Could this cowboy begin to understand what that meant to an abandoned teen? Though she hadn't done much research on Crew Ashman, she did know he'd been born and raised on one of the largest ranches in Arizona.

He leaned over the desk and began writing something in his ledger. "How much?" he asked. "I'll be happy to make a donation."

Tara's gaze fell to the desk, seeing for the first time that the ledger was actually a book of checks. "You think I came here for money?" Her cheeks were no doubt bright red again.

Ashman's hand stilled as he looked up at her with those gorgeous brown eyes. "You aren't here for a donation?"

She knew Lily would somehow change things to walk out of here with both a check and what she'd really come here for, but Tara had never been good at face-to-face requests. Give her social media, or even the phone, and she could ask for the world. In fact, she'd often done so to raise money for Lily's House over the years to help pay expenses for the girls who didn't receive funds from the state. But asking for favors in person was too much like begging. It opened you up for rejection.

"We need horses," she blurted. "We have a couple girls who are crazy about them, and we wanted to give them the opportunity to learn more about proper training." This was not working out at all the way she'd planned. After being rejected at just about every stable in town, as well as High Vista Farm, the Silver A Ranch was her last hope.

"So you want to buy a horse?" When she didn't reply right away, his eyes widened in understanding. "Oh, you want me to donate a horse. Well, I—"

"No!" She took a step back, her hands out in front of her in a holding motion. Why couldn't she seem to string a decent sentence together in his presence? "Tessa—that's Lily's sister, the psychologist—has two horses, and she lets the girls take care of them and even ride them, but we'd like to know if two girls could come here and volunteer. You don't have to pay them anything. Just let them feed the horses, curry them, whatever. They've worked with Tessa's horses and they were interested in horses even before they came to Lily's House, so they aren't complete novices. And they're good girls. They just need more than we can offer—horse-wise, that is."

He straightened, his eyes not leaving her face. "You want me to train them."

"Well, not exactly. They don't know everything, so they will need some instruction. Maybe they'll need a little attention . . ." She fell silent.

On the way over, she'd practiced everything she wanted to say, down to a not-so-subtle suggestion that she was doing him a favor by highlighting all the things the girls could do to help him, but he'd seen right through her. Her carefully planned speech had dissolved into a mess of emotion careening inside her body, because the fact was that the girls would need a lot of help learning the ropes, especially at first. If what Dervin King at High Vista had indicated was true about the Silver A Ranch being in trouble financially, Crew Ashman wouldn't be interested in taking on another burden.

But she was not without a backup plan, because this *would* be good for the girls and also the Silver A in the long run if they were trained. She knew it. "It's also good publicity," she said. "It'll create goodwill with the community."

He folded his arms. "Is that what you told Dervin at High Vista?"

She didn't respond but was sure her color had deepened. Mr. King had told her bluntly that he didn't have time to babysit, that he had to focus on beating his competitors.

"I'm not too sure the community would ever know about it," Crew added. "Or even just the horse community, for that matter. Not that I'm looking for that kind of publicity, mind you. I'm just pointing out that it's not really a plus."

"Well, it would be if you had a decent social media presence."

He blinked at her, as if she had begun speaking a foreign language he'd never heard before. "We have a Facebook page."

"That you haven't posted on since mid-March—over three months ago," she retorted. Now that she'd opened the door, she might as well plunge all the way in. "You need to be posting daily on Facebook. Twitter could be more than that. And you don't even have Pinterest or Instagram. With all these animals here, you could do some amazing posts."

His smile widened. "What would we post? We put up the breeding and training fees, and how many boarding openings we have. The rest, including our beef prices, is on our website."

"Which admittedly is a decent website," she said. Not nearly as flashy as High Vista's, but user friendly. "If you took out a few ads and did more interesting posts, you'd have horse lovers all over the world following you. Then you'd be the most popular breeding and training facility in the entire state, and maybe half the US."

Unexpectedly, he threw back his head and laughed. "I don't think social media has that kind of power. People know where we're at and what we sell. Besides, like I told you before, my main interest is my cattle, and I have established customers who don't shop on Facebook."

She pulled out the big guns. "High Vista Farm has forty thousand likes on their page. That's forty thousand horse lovers who see their posts but never see yours. I work for a marketing firm, and building strong social media profiles is one of the first things we do. I know it works."

He closed the book of checks and slipped it back into the drawer. "And just when am I supposed to do these posts? I have two full-time jobs here as it is."

She wanted to suggest that he hire someone, but if the Silver A Ranch was hurting financially, getting him to believe the money would be worth it might be a bigger challenge than accepting the girls. "Even a little bit can increase the page reach dramatically. And maybe the girls can help with taking pictures or coming up with fun ideas. Posts don't always have to be strictly horse related. High Vista posted a picture of a newborn giraffe last spring before the foaling started. They got thousands of shares." Which meant even more people saw it. Did he even know how Facebook worked?

His eyes roamed her face. He was more attractive this close—rugged, strong, determined. A man who might be real enough to stick around.

Stop, she told herself. She wasn't here for a romantic connection. If she wanted romance, she'd accept a date from one of the dozen guys she worked with. She only didn't because she knew too well from observation that they'd lose interest and chase after some pencil in a skirt the minute they grew bored.

Crew's look intensified. Time stretched between them, seeming almost to stop. Tara wanted desperately to flee, but she stood her ground, meeting his gaze, lifting her chin slightly in challenge.

"Okay," he said slowly. "Pending approval of my stable manager, I'll let the girls come, but they have to do at least ten hours a week on a regular schedule. Twenty would be better. Since it's summer and all."

Relief flooded Tara. She couldn't help the smile growing on her face. She'd succeeded!

"But I do have one condition," he added, his dark eyes glinting.

Her hopes plummeted. "And that is?" She hoped he didn't want her to accompany the girls because her marketing job already required fifty or sixty hours a week, and volunteering at Lily's took up the rest of her days. Yet at the same time, having him ask for her company would be flattering and a little bit exciting.

"For every week they're here, you'll spend two hours updating our social media pages." A mocking grin filled his face, and she had the distinct feeling he was toying with her.

Two hours? Well, it wasn't as if she couldn't carve out that much time. She'd have to cut back on helping out at Lily's House, or her sleep, or maybe stand up to her boss about the unpaid overtime, but the exchange for the girls would be worth it.

"Deal," she said before he could change his mind. She

proffered a hand to seal the agreement—didn't cowboys always shake on things? He took her hand and the sensation she'd experienced earlier infused her once again.

Totally my imagination, she thought. But he was watching her, his expression shuttered. For several heartbeats he didn't let go of her hand, and she didn't pull away. Finally, as if by mutual agreement, their hands dropped.

I do not like cowboys, Tara reminded herself again. She'd say it a million times if she had to. The truth was, his being a cowboy didn't make her leery, it was her reaction to him she distrusted. That was easily solved, though. She absolutely wouldn't go out with him, even if he asked. Not that he would ask, but now she didn't have to worry about it. She felt relief in making the decision.

"Let's go," he said.

"Go?" The way he'd spoken didn't sound like he meant for her to leave. Besides, they still had to discuss what time the girls would come.

His left eyebrow angled up in that same incredibly attractive way she'd noted before. "I'm sure you'd like to learn what I plan to have the girls do. And if you're going to be posting about my ranch, you need a tour to cover the basics."

Was he serious? She was wearing a suit, for crying out loud, one with a skirt. And her heels had already shown they were a problem. She looked at her feet, and lifted one heel. "Maybe I can come back with the girls."

"Not a problem. Wait right here." Going around the other side of the desk, he disappeared through an inner door.

She shook her head, unable to guess at his meaning.

As she glanced around the room, wishing he'd been more clear, her gaze snagged on a painting of an older couple behind his desk. His parents maybe? Or grandparents? She stepped closer for further investigation. The man looked like an older version of Crew.

"My grandparents," Crew said, startling her.

She turned around to see that he was carrying a pair of bright blue cowboy boots. "You gotta be kidding," she said before she could stop herself. No way was she putting on those ridiculous things.

He gave her a slow smile that made her heart do a little dance. "Why not? They match your suit. I brought socks too."

He held out both the boots and socks, a challenge in his eyes. But it was the amusement she also saw there that made her take them from his hands. She sat in one of the two chairs in front of the desk and traded her black heels for the boots. To her surprise, the leather, while not exactly soft, was pliable. They were only the slightest bit too large.

She looked up to see him staring at her, an odd expression on his handsome face—lost, maybe. Definitely sad. Both of these emotions she understood too well. Who did these boots belong to that seeing her in them brought that look to his face?

2

Crew dragged his attention from the boots, forcing a smile as he offered Tara his hand. "Shall we?"

"Sure."

Her hand was soft in his rough one, and it called up a yearning inside him that he hadn't felt in a long time. Even before Dervin King showed up three years ago and started High Vista Farm with his rich daddy's money, there had been no time in his life for anything but work. The struggle to hold onto what his grandfather had built, and what his father had almost destroyed, was constant. Another year should tell if the Silver A Ranch's fifty-year legacy would continue or if he'd have to close down the stables altogether, sell some land, and cut his cattle business in half. Crew wouldn't make the decision lightly since he had employees, most of them extended family, that depended on him for a living.

Whatever happened, he wouldn't sell Iron Express to High Vista and consign him to a life of continuous forced breeding. Thanks to his father, Dervin already had Jump Start. Sophie had never forgiven him for not being able to prevent that.

"Where are we going?" Tara asked as they left the office.

He liked the flavor of her voice, deeper than most women but soft like silk. He liked even more the blue eyes and the unruly black mane that reminded him of his best show mares. "First the stables where you found me. Are the boots okay?"

"Yes, thank you. Is that where you keep the horses you train?" She kept up with him easily, which was surprising since his employees were always telling him he walked too fast. To be sure, she wasn't a wisp of a girl like so many women these days, and he found his eyes drawn to her womanly curves in that blue suit more than he wanted to admit.

"It's for those we board, as well as holding stalls for those that come here only for training. We call it the training stables among ourselves, but it's really the only stables anyone else sees, which is why it's closest to the training fields and the parking lot. Of course, we don't train all the horses we board. Some of their owners do that on their own. We also have separate facilities for our workhorses, brood mares, mares with foals, and yearlings. Keeping them separate limits diseases."

He walked her through the corridor of the barn and was pleased when several of the horses came to investigate, putting their long faces over their stall doors. Tara stopped to pet one of them, her hand running over the mare's black coat.

"She's beautiful," she murmured, laughing when the horse nuzzled her face.

"So, you're not afraid of horses."

She smiled. "I've ridden before. Actually, quite a lot in my teens. Though nothing as expensive as I bet this horse is."

"Her sire is Iron Express, and just the stud fee to create her was seventy thousand, so I'd say she's one of the most expensive kind."

She whistled. "I had no idea they cost so much. Thank you again for letting the girls come."

The last thing he needed was to spend time teaching two rebellious teenage girls how to take care of horses, but at the same time, he knew he couldn't turn them away. Because Sophie was somewhere out there, and he'd want someone to help her, if she reached out to anyone.

"We'll work them hard," he warned. "Everyone here works hard. They may not like it."

Tara laughed. "That's perfect. There's only one thing that Lily gives out more than chores to the girls, and that's love." Again the melancholy expression he'd caught earlier on her face. This beautiful, incredibly sexy woman had a connection to Lily's House that he didn't yet understand. But he intended to. She was interesting and determined, a combination he found irresistible.

"We have about ten stalls open at the moment," he said, trying not to let the anger his admission caused show in his voice. One more thing that his father and High Vista were responsible for. While the Silver A had never depended on the horse training side of the business for its main income, it had always turned a profit until his father took his shares and went into business with High Vista. With the losses in Crew's cattle at the same time, things had been difficult these past three years.

Too bad this woman's social media ideas wouldn't be helpful. His horse clients didn't care about cute memes or posts about giraffes, whatever she thought. They came here only because of Iron Express's reputation and the trainers he'd hired. All Crew wanted to focus on now was rebuilding so he could keep the horses.

Because when Sophie returned—if she returned—he wanted the Thoroughbreds here for her.

"The girls will start out working with our mares and foals and yearlings," he said. "Mostly those intended to be workhorses. If they do well, I'll move them to helping out here, feeding and exercising the animals whose owners don't come in daily to do that themselves. Of course, I can't have them riding the horses until they're certified, but they can lead them around."

"I can understand that. In fact, knowing how expensive these horses are, I think I'd feel better if they only helped out with your workhorses. No wonder even the smaller stables turned me down. Their Thoroughbreds might not be as prestigious as yours, but I'm betting they still cost a lot of money."

He laughed at her grimace. She had the kind of face that showed her emotion, and he found her honesty refreshing. "We'll make sure the girls learn what they need to work with all the horses. In the meantime, we have plenty of foals here for the girls to love and spend time with, both workhorses and Thoroughbreds. We like to have them handled as much as possible so they grow up to be friendly."

"I'd love to see the foals."

Her smile sent sunshine into him. Her eyes had taken on a darker blue inside the barn, closer to the color of her suit. He found it hard to look away. "Come on, then, I'll show you."

"Are we walking or driving?" she asked.

He should take his truck, because he had a million things he needed to do and time was always important. But he wanted to walk across the fields with her, especially now that she'd gotten rid of those ridiculous high heels, even if the boots did cover up her attractive calves. "Walking, if you don't mind."

Her hands went to the buttons of her suit coat. "I'll have to leave this in my car then. It's a little hot out."

Blistering, in fact. "We can drive, if you prefer." He watched as she finished undoing the buttons and slipped off the jacket. Underneath was a silky black tank that made his throat turn dry.

"Walking's fine. I don't have any other place to be. I took the day off work."

When was the last time he'd taken a day off? He couldn't remember. Well, he'd gone for drinks with some of the hands a couple weeks ago. He'd been so busy saving the ranch that nothing else mattered.

Except for Sophie, of course. Maybe it was time to hire an investigator to look for her. Maybe enough time had passed that she would listen to him.

"There's an office here at the stable where we can leave your jacket," he said. "It's my stable manager's but he won't mind."

They left the jacket in the deserted office and started down a cement walkway that soon gave way to a narrow, grass-covered road that meandered through the fields. "The boots still okay?" he asked after a moment.

She laughed, revealing a dimple on her right cheek that hadn't appeared during the initial stiffness between them. "Yeah. They're actually comfortable." She looked like she wanted to say something more about the boots, but she didn't.

They left the training areas behind them and reached a field the boarding horses used for exercise and grazing. "It's beautiful," Tara said, admiring the land that wasn't yet seared from the summer heat. "How long has your family lived here?"

"My great-grandfather bought most of this land almost a hundred years ago, but his father also herded cattle here before that. We've worked hard to preserve the natural vegetation that tends to be less dependent on water."

"Seems pretty green. I mean, for Arizona."

"Well, it's only June. But we have water rights and wells, so we keep a close eye on what's going on in the pastures. We also have a contract for grazing on federal land, which helps."

They walked a few more minutes in silence, and he found himself thinking of things to say that might bring back her smile and that dimple.

"It's summer, so do you have any preferred hours?" she asked as they approached a field with two Thoroughbred mares and their foals. "One of the girls is seventeen, so she'll be driving them both in Lily's van. But in the fall, they'll have school, of course."

He didn't miss the indication that she hoped they'd continue after school started. They'd better stay at least that long if he invested the time in them. That made him brood—what was he doing getting himself into this?

"Oh, look at that!" Tara was gazing into the field they'd reached, where two black Thoroughbred foals were chasing each other around, jumping awkwardly into the air. "They're beautiful. Their mothers too."

"They should be. They've got a pedigree as long as my arm." Both the foals had been sired by Iron Express, but the gray mare's sire was Jump Start, and her foal looked remarkably like Jump Start had at the same age. For three years, he'd bred this gray mare, hoping for this foal and finally, here he was. Her two other foals had been fillies.

"I take it these aren't the workhorses."

"No, those are in the next field. These mares are Thoroughbreds. Most of the Thoroughbred breeding we do is with outside mares, and their owners take them home after, but the foals are fun to have around, so we birth some every year and sell them after they're weaned. Helps pay for their upkeep. I'd take you to meet them if you weren't wearing a skirt. The gate is over by that little barn. But let's see if they come over when I call."

In answer, she stepped up on the rail of the fence and boosted herself up until she was sitting on the fence. Then, angling away from him, she pulled her legs up together, swinging them over. "Easy."

A deep chuckle filled his chest. "Okay then."

She smirked. "I do well with challenges."

"I'll remember that." He climbed over himself, whistling to the mares. One of them whinnied, and both came galloping over, their foals following awkwardly. He wished he'd thought to grab a carrot to let Tara give them a treat.

"I've never seen that color before," she said, watching the gray mare. "She's silver, or something."

"She's called a gray, and what that means is her skin is black and her coat mostly white. They often change color with their age, graying more. She always has gray offspring, so though her foal is black now, he'll eventually start turning gray, maybe at a year."

"She's beautiful."

The mares had reached them now, both ignoring Tara and extending their noses to him. He ran his hands over both of them at the same time. The chestnut horse was shyer than the gray, but both were docile and affectionate creatures.

One of the foals miscalculated his steps and bumped into Tara. "Oh, it's adorable," she said.

"That one's a filly. Name's Iron Queen. She's already sold but will be here until she weans. We're never in a hurry for that here, so it'll be a few more months."

"And the other?"

"He's the gray—or will be. Doesn't have an official name yet, but I call him JS Junior, for short, after his grandsire. He'll get another name once he has an owner." Crew wouldn't be selling him, though she didn't have to know that.

"Nice. They're so friendly."

"We work hard on imprinting directly after their birth. And they're handled every day."

"Big investment of time."

He smiled. "A lot like the girls at your Lily's House, I imagine."

She tilted her head upwards to look at him, her hair shining in the sun. "Yes. And worth every bit. Thank you for doing this."

"You're welcome." Time froze between them. Crew would give almost anything to lean over and kiss her. The thought pulled him up short. What was he thinking? She was only at the ranch for a favor, and kissing her would be totally inappropriate.

Still, she didn't wear a wedding ring, and she didn't seem in an awful hurry to leave.

They fondled the colts for a while until they wandered off, chasing each other again. Tara took out her phone from some hidden pocket and began to snap photographs. Crew stared after the colts. If Sophie could see them now. He looked up to find Tara snapping a picture of him.

When he started to protest, she smiled—without the dimple this time—and said, "It's for Facebook."

"Oh, right." He gave a farewell rub to each of the mares and started back to the fence. They'd barely jumped it when his phone rang. It was Isaac Kelley, his cousin on his mother's side, and his ranch manager.

"Hey, Isaac, what's up?" He hoped it wasn't anything bad. Isaac was twenty years older than he was and had been part of the ranch since before he'd been born, so the fact that Isaac was calling him when he was out with the cows meant something couldn't wait.

"I'm sending you a picture," Isaac said. "Lookee what I found."

"Just a minute." Crew pulled up the picture of Isaac with a newborn calf in his arms. Through the phone, he could hear a cow bawling, obviously angry at the separation from her baby. He put his phone back to his ear. "They've started calving then."

"Yep. First one."

"Is he as small as he looks, or are you going through a sudden growth spurt?"

Most of the ranch calves were born in the late winter or early spring and sold in the fall, but Crew had set up a test group to give birth during the summer to see if the calves were healthier. It meant he'd have to winter them instead of selling them in the fall, and then sell them in late summer next year. The lack of competition at that time should send his beef prices skyrocketing. He hoped.

Isaac laughed. "He's tiny, which is why I'm bringing him and his momma in to keep an eye on. He's a twin, though, so he's actually big. Both of them'll be fine."

Twins! That was a different story. Unlike horses, cattle often had successful multiple births. "Great. I'll meet you there in a bit." The cow had stopped bawling, so she must be in the van with her calves now. Good thing they'd moved them in closer from their more wild terrain last week.

"Good news?" Tara asked when he hung up the phone.

"Twins," he said. "First births of the summer. It's a good omen." His grin faded. "I know we were going on to see the other foals but I really need to check on these calves and on rest of that herd—"

"Fine. Raincheck."

Did she really mean it? He wanted to pin her down to a time now, but that felt awkward.

They turned and began walking back the way they'd come. "When should the girls be here?" she asked. "We never decided."

"How about eight in the morning?" That was three hours after his day normally began. The delay would give him a chance to check for new calves born in the night and time to repair a broken fence he'd jury-rigged yesterday before he'd have to come down from the fields to meet the girls.

He still needed to talk to the stable manager about them coming, but that was a matter of formality since they'd be working with the workhorses in the beginning.

"Tomorrow. Oh, good." Tara sounded a bit surprised. "They can get up that early, can't they?"

Her laugh was genuine. "I'm glad that's Lily's problem, not mine. She's a whole lot scarier than me. In a good way. She'll make it work. Anything they should wear?"

"Comfortable clothes and lots and lots of sun screen."

At the training stables, they retrieved her jacket. "About the social media pages," she said. "I'll need someone to give me access."

He was tempted to tell her to forget social media, that he'd just been teasing, but it was an easy way to get her phone number. "If you give me your number, I'll call you about it."

She pulled a business card from the pocket of the jacket lying over her arm.

"Thank you." He took the card without looking at it. "So, do you want to go for a ride some time?" There, he'd said it, but why had he asked her to go for a ride? She'd probably rather go out for a drink or dinner.

Her expressive face went blank, as if she'd slammed a door. Not a glimpse of pleasure or excitement or even revulsion. A pit formed in his gut. He'd been so sure that there was a connection between them, but it was possible he'd misread things. Focusing on work hadn't exactly given him practice with dating. Why hadn't he kept his stupid mouth shut?

"I'd like that," she said after a hesitation that felt like a year to him. "And I'd like to see those calves, if I could. I don't think I've ever seen a baby cow."

The tension slid out of him. "Sure. I'll give you a call."

He watched her walk down to the parking lot and get into her car. She was one fine woman. Yet something was off about the scene, and it wasn't until she'd disappeared and he was halfway to the east cow field on his horse that he realized what it was.

She'd still been wearing the blue boots, and he needed them back.

3

Tara ran inside the front door at Lily's House at full speed without knocking. "Lily!" she called. "I did it! I found a place for the girls to work with horses."

Lily appeared, her blond hair swept up into a ponytail. "That's great! Was it the place you were hoping for?"

"Well, no. It wasn't. Or any of the ones on the list I made, but one recommended another and so on, until I finally ended up at the Silver A Ranch."

Lily whooped with her before tugging her into the kitchen were dinner was already simmering on the stove. Two foster girls at the long table greeted at her before going back to one of the puzzles Lily always kept going somewhere in the house.

"The Silver A Ranch," Lily mused. "That's a cattle farm, right? So will the girls be working with their ranch horses, or do they offer riding lessons or something as well?"

"They actually have workhorses and Thoroughbreds, and offer horse training, so I think it's perfect. There'll be a lot of opportunities to learn different things. But how'd you know they raise cattle?"

"I buy my beef in bulk from a butcher who buys cattle from them. He says they're the best in the area. And their meat doesn't have hormones."

Leave it to Lily to know that. Tara smiled. "The owner seems rather nice. Well, once he realized I wasn't from his competitor."

Lily made a face. "Was he rude before that?"

"No. Just very coldly polite." As close as they were, she wasn't going to tell Lily about how attractive she'd found him. She hadn't even meant to accept his offer of going for a ride. In fact, she'd told herself to refuse, but somehow she hadn't been able to. She wanted to see more of him.

"Oh, well." Lily stirred her soup. "I'll have to go meet him for myself."

She was probably wondering if he might donate a side or two of beef for the girls. "I was sure you would."

"So aren't you going to tell Kate and Brin?"

"Where are they?"

Lily's laugh rang throughout the kitchen. "You have to ask?"

Tara found the girls out in the barn with Tessa's horse Serenity. Kate Miller, the seventeen-year-old, was currying her, while Brin Thompson, who was two years younger, perched on top of the stall wall, her thin legs dangling down. As usual, a piece of her straggly blond hair was in her mouth. They both looked up when they noticed Tara standing outside the stall.

"You did it!" Kate dropped the curry brush and rushed over to the stall door. "Where? What kind of horses? Did they say we could ride them?" Kate's short hair was dyed black and her round face layered with pale makeup. Black lipstick and thick black rings around her eyes completed what Tara called her mask. She was slightly on the chubby side, which was emphasized by pants so tight, it was a wonder they didn't burst. Lily limited few things in self-expression regarding hair and makeup and even clothes as long as they covered the most important parts. Only piercings and tattoos were out of the question until they were eighteen. Lily enforced that as religiously as she did her no-swearing rule.

"Yep! I found you a place."

"Where?" the girls asked together. Brin jumped down from the stall and hurried over, her narrow face eager. She was the quietest and most introverted of Lily's girls, and it was good to see her this excited.

"Silver A Ranch," Tara said.

Kate's eyes widened. "You mean the one who owns Iron Express? No way! He won like a zillion races and his offspring are always placing at the top. That's amazing!" She pumped her fist and then slapped a high five with Brin.

"You've heard of them?" Tara asked.

"Well, yeah. Of course I have. Anyone interested in horses knows who they are."

Brin nodded her agreement without speaking.

"They aren't a huge operation," Kate went on, "but before High Vista showed up a couple years ago, they were bigger. I'm not sure how it happened, but somehow High Vista ended up with some of their horses. It was all news back then."

That had been before either of the girls had come to live at Lily's House. "Okay, I'm glad you're happy about it, but you girls will need to be there at eight every morning."

Kate gawked. "Are you kidding?"

"Hey, that's when they need you. The owner gets up at five."

"Well, that's what I mean. It's late for a ranch."

Tara rolled her eyes. "This from the girl Lily has to force out of bed on school mornings."

"That's different. These are Thoroughbreds."

Kate looked so happy, Tara hated to say, "They won't start you out with the Thoroughbreds. You know that, right? Certainly not riding them. Those horses cost a fortune."

Kate and Brin exchanged a look and Kate said, "Yeah, we talked about that. We don't care how much poop we have to shovel, we're going to do it."

All the hassles of the day were worth it for that moment. "Wait. I need to record you saying that on my phone. Come out here."

That led to the girls oohing and ahhing over her pictures of the baby colts—and over her picture of Crew Ashman.

"He is the most beautiful cowboy I've ever seen," Kate said with a sigh.

Tara laughed. "I think he's rugged."

"Yes, rugged," Brin said. "By the way, Tara, where did you get those boots? I thought you hated cowboy boots."

Tara stared down at the ground to see three pair of feet shod in boots. "Oops. Yeah, I borrowed these while I was there so I could go on a mini tour. I forgot my shoes." Leave it to the quiet Brin to notice. How embarrassing.

"They're cute, and they match your skirt." Kate bent down for a closer look. "We can take them back for you."

"Thanks. I'll let you know." Tara would prefer to deliver them herself to make sure they got back safely. She had no idea who they belonged to, but they meant something to Crew.

The girls were going back inside the stall where Serenity was investigating the curry brush. "So you'll be there on time?" she asked the girls.

Brin twirled a piece of her hair. "I'll make sure she's up." The hair went promptly into her mouth.

"Oh, yeah," Tara added. "He said wear comfortable clothes and lots of sun screen. You should probably tie back your hair, too." She grinned. "Keep the poop out."

The girls giggled, but Brin didn't stop chewing on her hair. It was part habit and part self-comforting, Lily said, and she didn't seem worried about it, so Tara wouldn't be either.

After stopping at the house one more time to make sure Lily knew what time the girls needed to be at the Silver A in the morning, Tara headed across town to the two-bedroom apartment she shared with another girl, Rylee Williams.

Tara sat down at the desk in the corner of her room. She knew her inbox would be full of questions she needed to answer. A day off for her didn't really mean a day off. It meant working from home later to take care of the clients. But she didn't turn on her computer. Instead, she pulled off the boots and studied them for a moment.

She was about to set them to the side when she noticed the small, neat writing on the inside near the top of each boot: Sophie Ashman.

Her heart flip-flopped. Sophie Ashman? She'd suspected the boots belonged to someone important to him, but he hadn't been wearing a ring. Was he divorced? Had this Sophie died? Or was he married but didn't wear a ring because it got in the way of his work? Maybe his asking her if she wanted to go for a ride meant something altogether different than how she'd taken it. Maybe, he meant with the girls or . . .

No, she'd seen the look in his eyes, and that look was the only reason she'd said yes.

She opened her laptop, but she didn't check her email. She had some investigating to do.

Silver A Ranch, she typed into her browser. *Let's see what the Internet has to say about you, Crew Ashman.*

4

Crew had checked for new calves, repaired the broken fence, and taken Iron Express for a short ride before eight o'clock. Iron Express was too valuable to ride hard, but they both still enjoyed their time together, and to make up for not riding as often or as far as Crew would have liked, he allowed the stallion plenty of field time.

He finished his ride at the training stables where he planned to meet the girls from Lily's House. To his surprise, the teens were already there waiting. An attractive woman with blond hair was with the two girls, and he recognized her from the Internet search he'd done the night before: Lily Perez. She looked happy and confident, and everything about her screamed reliability.

Unfortunately, the girls with her looked far from the "good girls" Tara had promised him. At least the plump one, who looked the type to hang out behind the school smoking pot. She did look strong enough to do the work on the ranch, which was more than he could say for the scrawny little wisp of a girl next to her, who appeared to be chewing on the ends of her ponytail.

Lily smiled at him as he swung down from Iron Express. "Are you Crew Ashman?"

"That would be me."

Lily opened her mouth to say more when the girl with all the makeup gave a gasp. "That's Iron Express, isn't it? Oh, wow, oh wow, oh wow! He's amazing!" She took a step toward the stallion, then hesitated, her gaze going to Crew. "Can I touch him?"

In that moment, she won him over. He recognized a true horse lover when he saw one.

"Sure, you can. Let him sniff you first." Crew signaled a passing groom. "Can you bring me a carrot?"

The groom hurried back with a carrot from the stash they kept inside the training stables. Crew broke it in pieces and gave them to the girls, who eagerly fed Iron Express the treat. Neither girl hesitated or acted afraid, and the near worship in their eyes was endearing. These two were something he could work with. It wasn't as if he didn't have other misfits on the ranch, and in the end, it hadn't made a difference. They all became family.

He looked over to find Lily watching him. "Thank you," she said, a knowing smile on her face. "I really appreciate this. Please let me know if I need to get the girls anything."

"Sure will." Crew touched his finger to his hat as Lily left. He turned to the girls. "So what are your names?"

"I'm Kate Miller, and she's Brin Thompson," the older girl said. "This is the most amazing day of my life. I never thought I'd ever touch a famous Thoroughbred."

Suddenly the morning he had planned for the girls cleaning out the boarding stalls under the watchful eye of the assistant stable manager wasn't at all what he wanted for them. Not for their first experience at the Silver A.

Crew gestured for the hovering groom to take Iron Express. He normally preferred to rub down his stallion himself after their rides, but today he'd arranged to let the groom handle it. The girls gave Iron Express one last pat before the man led him away.

"Come on, girls," Crew said. "Let me show you your first responsibility. It's something you'll need to do every morning."

He drove them in his truck past the field with the Thoroughbred foals to where a half dozen other foals played with their mothers in a larger field. "They're so cute," whispered Brin. The first words he'd heard from her.

A thin, gray-haired cowboy was already setting up in the nearby stable. "Benjamin," Crew called to him. "I brought you some helpers this morning."

Old Benjamin was one of the most patient and thorough of his stablemen, and he was over the care of all the workhorses. "That'll be great," he said. "I need to re-shoe the mares today, so I could use help with the babies."

Crew stayed long enough to see the girls inside a stall, brushing and petting a foal, while Benjamin and its mother watched. The delight in the girls' faces reminded him of the first day Sophie had laid eyes on Jump Start.

Clenching his jaw against the emotion, he started to turn. But Kate arose and came toward him, her movements slow enough not to startle the foal. "Thank you," she said, her ringed eyes earnest.

He dipped his head. "Don't thank me yet, you're cleaning out stalls next."

"That's okay," she said with a laugh. She started to turn but stopped and added, "Do you think . . . do you think we might ever ride one of the Thoroughbreds? Or work with them?" The longing in her expression was apparent. Behind her, Brin was watching them, her hands still brushing the little foal.

He brought his gaze to Kate's, holding it for a few second before replying. "It's not me you have to impress but Benjamin and all the others in charge of the horses. But I'll tell you what, Kate. You give me your best, and I can promise you that within a month, you'll get your wish. Deal?"

Her head bounced up and down, her eyes shining. "Deal!"

With a bounce in his step that hadn't been there this morning, Crew left the barn. It had been the right thing to do, letting them come.

He didn't see the girls before they left at noon because he was out helping Isaac and the others move the cows to another pasture. Rotating the cattle was the best way they had to ensure the grasses would regrow and last throughout the season. After moving the cattle, they had to check the fence lines again to make sure there were no breaks in the new pasture. They found a cow that was stuck in a pond, and it took three of them to get her out. At the end of their adventure, he was covered in mud.

By the time he rode back to Isaacs's house for dinner at six-thirty, the three ranch hands who boarded on the Silver A had finished eating and either gone into town or headed back to their bunkhouse. The employees who didn't board— most of those who worked with the Thoroughbreds—were probably long gone to their own houses, even the stable manager. Only Isaac, the ranch manager, was still out with the cows.

Crew scrubbed his hands and face at the outdoor water pump, surprising a few chickens pecking at the ground nearby. He sat down at the long outdoor table with a thankful sigh. Normally when he was late, he'd go inside and get his own food, but Julie Kelley, Isaac's wife, wouldn't appreciate the dried mud on his boots and pants.

Being here was familiar and comfortable, and he felt himself relaxing. He'd grown up in this house, but ten years ago when they'd built the training stables, they'd also built the new house. Breeding and training Thoroughbreds was all about appearances, his grandfather had said, and folks who dropped seventy grand on a stud fee expected a wealthy atmosphere. The new house had been the one thing his father and grandfather hadn't argued about. Now Crew was the only one who lived there.

Like the men who boarded, Crew always ate at Isaac and Julie's. Julie was a fabulous cook, and it was good to unwind before heading home. If he didn't eat here, for whatever reason, he was more likely to fall into bed without eating and watch TV until he slept.

Julie emerged from the house and set a large bowl of stew and a plate with two biscuits in front of him. "Extra biscuit?"

He smiled wearily as he removed his hat and placed it next to the bowl. "You know it. Thanks."

She set her hand on his shoulder. "You work too hard."

"We could say the same about Isaac. He's back out with the cows."

She laughed. "He's a stubborn old fool. But maybe once we're past the danger."

The danger of losing everything because of what his father had done. Isaac, as the ranch manager, might be an employee, but he was also a shareholder, and Crew considered him a partner.

"I'll make sure he rests then," he told Julie. For as long as he remembered, Julie had been here on the ranch, and after his grandmother had gone, followed by his mother, Julie had been a mother figure for him.

Marti, Isaac's adult daughter, emerged from the house, opening a Dr. Pepper and setting it in front of him. The sun hung low in the sky, glinting through her red hair. "Hard day?"

"Less than usual," he said. But he did feel tired. Bone tired.

Marti sat down next to him, far enough away so she didn't touch his mud-caked leg. "Poor baby," she said, pushing out her bottom lip. "What you need is a little more fun in your life."

"Maybe." He shoveled in a few more bites.

She laughed. "You know I'm right." She chatted on about all the fun things he could do as he only half listened.

Marti could rope and ride as well as any cowboy, but she planned to become a veterinarian. Someday he'd hire her full time. He occasionally found himself wishing she weren't his second cousin who seemed more like a little sister because it would be a darn sight easier to marry a cowgirl like her than go out and find someone who was suited for this life. At twenty-two, she was six years younger than he was, but that wasn't much.

"So how's college?" he asked her when he was almost finished with his stew.

"Good. Really good." She watched him eat for a few more minutes before adding, "I met someone last week. We've been out three times since. Name's Trevor Hadfield."

He stopped chewing. "And?"

"I think I'm going to marry him."

"Don't you think it's a little soon to be picking out china and debating baby names?"

"Sometimes one look is all it takes."

Crew had a sudden vision of walking out of the training stables to see Tara Levine staring at him. He also thought about how she'd acted around the Thoroughbred foals.

"Crew?" Marti bent over to look at him.

He shook his head to clear it. "Sorry. Been a long day." He guzzled his drink, folded his two biscuits in a napkin, and stood. "I'd better get home. I wanted to look over the books again."

She jumped up from the table. "I'll walk with you. I don't get to see you enough. I'd been planning to ask you to go for a ride tonight, but I can see that ain't going to happen. What you need is a nice hot bath."

That did sound good, and heaven knew his jetted tub was comfortable.

She laughed at his blissful expression. "Guess I'll settle for walking you home."

Crew was glad for the company. As a child, she and Sophie had tagged along behind him everywhere. Sometimes he'd been annoyed, but when they'd finally grown up, they'd all been friends. His house was only a half mile away, and they walked along the grassy back road in silence as he munched on his biscuits. There had probably been cake too, but he wasn't going back for a slice now.

They talked about casual things, laughing about her experiences at school and how he'd ended up covered in mud. When they reached his back lawn, Marti stopped and turned to him, her face serious. "So what are you going to do about the gray foal? You've finally got him. Now what?"

He didn't know, plain and simple. He'd bred that gray foal for Sophie, but he had no idea how to reach her or where she was.

"It's time," Marti said, taking his free hand. "I miss her too. She was my best friend."

The words bit at him, because despite the four years between him and Sophie, she had been *his* best friend and he had been hers. Even before Marti. They'd been motherless and grandmotherless. No children knew loss the way they did.

"She wasn't your best friend," he shot back, pulling his hand away. "And she wasn't mine. Or she wouldn't have run away."

"She was hurting," Marti said.

Unbidden fury swept through him. "So was I! I didn't leave her."

"That's because you're responsible, and she was still a kid. Besides, you had Iron Express."

He turned away, pacing. "I'd have given him up a million times for her. I'd have given up this whole ranch!"

"You don't mean that."

He faced her. "Even when my father gave Jump Start and the other horses to High Vista. When he gave our land to them. When he caused the death of two hundred head of cattle—or four hundred if you also count the unborn calves—because he wanted the money to drink himself to death. Never mind what Grandpa had wanted. Never mind that he screwed me and your dad. Never mind that he broke Sophie's heart. Even when he did all that, we came away stronger. All of us. All of us but Sophie. I was still here. You were still here. Your parents were still here. We're family, all of us fighting for the ranch together, but she threw us away. And don't tell me again that she was a kid. She was barely younger than you are now."

He didn't realize his hurt had grown into such anger. Was it only yesterday he'd thought about hiring another investigator to find Sophie? Not a day had gone by when he hadn't thought about his sister, wondering if she was dead in a ditch or if she'd found a safe place to land. Three years of not knowing. That was what hurt most of all. Because his sister was out there somewhere, and he couldn't take care of her. If she was alive, she probably still hated him for not saving Jump Start. Failing her and his grandfather hurt more than Crew could admit, even to Marti.

"Maybe that's the curse of my family," he said, his tongue tasting like acid. "Maybe all the women are destined to leave."

"Hey, I'm a woman in this family," Marti retorted. "Just because your mother couldn't hack it here doesn't mean the rest of us will leave. I will never leave the Silver A. I love it here."

Crew's anger slid from him at the hurt in his cousin's eyes. "I'm sorry. I'm out of line."

"You sure are." Marti glared at him for several seconds before closing the gap between them, reaching up to pull his forehead down to hers, nearly tipping off his hat. "Sophie will come back when she's ready."

Again the fury and betrayal welled up inside him, but he fought it down. "I no longer care if she ever comes back."

His attempt didn't fool Marti. "Does that mean you're selling the foal?" When he didn't respond, she laughed softly and said, "I didn't think so. You'd better get rid of that anger before she does come back, or you'll scare her away."

"Go home, Marti." He lifted his head from hers.

She nodded. "You need more fun. Remember that."

With a kiss on his cheek, she turned and strode across the grass, walking like the rancher she was. Tears threatened as he recalled Sophie walking the same way, but he squelched the emotion as he had so many times since she'd left. As of this moment, he was going to follow Marti's recommendation and find some fun.

No sooner had the thought come to his mind than his eyes caught something out of his peripheral vision. He rotated to face the newcomer and felt a tightening in his chest as he saw Tara Levine strolling toward him across the grass. She was wearing jean shorts that made her legs look as if they went on forever, and her red blouse set off her ample curves perfectly. She flipped her long hair over her shoulder and gave him a tentative smile. She was gorgeous.

As if he'd stepped from the darkness into the sunshine, all anger left and his weariness vanished. This night had just gotten a whole lot better.

5

Tara had sat in the parking lot at the Silver A Ranch for fifteen minutes, debating if she should use the small connecting road that wound up to the front of Crew's house instead of leaving her car in the regular parking lot. Using that parking lot meant approaching the house from the rear, and that felt a little like intrusion, despite the light burning inside his office at the back of the house. As she debated, she'd seen a of couple workers going in and out of the training stables, and one woman had come to drop off her horse. Compared to yesterday, the parking lot was almost deserted.

Finally, she grabbed the boots by the tops and decided to walk up the pathway from the parking lot and knock on his office door. She was halfway up the cement path when she heard voices arguing. The next step brought her into view of a couple behind the gazebo that sat a short distance from Crew's back deck. It was Crew with a fiery-haired woman.

Tara hesitated as the voices raised in anger and then lowered. Finally, the couple stood in an oddly intimate moment, forehead to forehead before the woman kissed Crew's cheek and sauntered away.

Maybe now wasn't a good time. Tara could come back later or let the girls return the boots for her after all.

No. She'd come all this way, and what did she care about the redhead? Crew had asked her to go for a ride, but that didn't mean he wasn't dating others. She certainly wasn't traipsing out here again just because she'd accidentally stumbled on a private moment between Crew and a beautiful woman.

So why did she feel so disappointed?

She took three more steps, and finally he turned toward her. A smile appeared on his face, sending tingles up her arms and through her chest. He was every bit as attractive as she remembered from yesterday.

"Hi there," he said as they both continued to close the gap. "What brings you out here? Don't tell me the girls are giving up already?" He hooked a thumb in one of his front pockets as he came to a stop.

She laughed. "No, they texted me a dozen times after they got home. They love it. In fact, they want to stay longer each day. I told them they needed to work at least a week before they asked to change anything." She held up the boots. "Anyway, I brought these back."

"Thank you." He reached out for the boots. "You'll have to excuse all the dirt. I wasn't expecting company."

She'd been far too busy staring into his eyes and losing herself in their brown depths to notice before, but now that he mentioned it, he did look like he'd walked through knee-deep mud at some point during the day.

"You only now finishing work?"

"Pretty much. Just came from dinner."

"I hope I'm not interrupting."

"Not at all."

Should she leave? What she really wanted to do was to ask him about what she'd found out on the Internet, specifically where his sister had vanished to, and how High Vista had ended up with Jump Start.

Lily always told her she liked to start at the end instead of taking the proper steps to get where she needed to go. That was also part of why dating didn't go well for her—she could always tell it would end terribly right from the start, so what was the purpose in giving it a decent try? The truth was that people left. They always left. Always. It was a lesson she'd learned very young.

Her excitement at learning that Sophie was Crew's sister and not a girlfriend or wife had puzzled her. In fact, she hadn't been able to stop smiling all day. All her coworkers had noticed. Perhaps it might only be a matter of time before she guessed at her "end" with Crew, but she hadn't glimpsed anything yet, so there was always the slightest chance this time would be different.

Meanwhile he stood there with those wide shoulders and eyes that drank her in like water.

"I came up with a few pictures and ideas for social media," she told him.

"Already?"

That made her laugh. "If you were my boss, you'd be asking what took me so long."

"Sounds like a winner."

"He's taught me a lot, but he is rather high strung."

"Well, come on in," he said. "If you don't mind waiting

a bit for me to clean up, I'll be happy to look at what you got."

She followed him through a door at the opposite end of the house which opened into a two-car garage. A shiny silver truck sat in the middle of the organized space. "Wherever you got muddy, you weren't in that truck," she said.

His laughter echoed heartily through the garage. "I have a beat-up Toyota I use on the ranch. This truck we use for regular life and to pull the horse trailer when we need to."

"You have a regular life?"

He laughed again. "Sometimes I wonder. Maybe none of us do." He reached up high and set the pair of blue boots on one of the shelves near the door where other shoes and boots were neatly arranged. Then he sat on the stair leading into the house and pulled off his own dirty boots, setting them on the floor under the shelves. "I lose more boots to cows in the mud than anything else," he said.

"They can't be cleaned?"

"Yes, but it's a pain. I'll do it later." He peeled his socks off, tossing them next to the boots, and then rolled up his pants a few turns, presumably to protect his flooring from the few remaining clumps of mud. Standing, he opened the door to the house for her, pushing it inward. "It involves a special cleaner and a little patience, is all."

Tara barely heard him. She was too busy looking around the amazing kitchen. Huge expanses of white cabinets, beautiful light fixtures hanging down from the ceiling on chains, an enormous center island with decorative shelves and a second sink, lovely gray-marbled granite countertops, an industrial-sized stainless steel stovetop, double ovens, and a glistening steel fridge. Everything was light and airy. It was a room to live and work in, yet it felt new and unused.

She came back to herself to find him staring at her. "You like to cook?" he asked.

"No. Well, I mean, I love the idea of cooking, but with working so much, I don't have the time, and of course my apartment isn't nearly this nice. What about you?" With a kitchen like this, he had to cook.

"I think about it every now and then but mostly by the end of the day, I just want to crash. My sister liked to cook." He broke off, his mouth puckering as if he'd tasted something sour.

"Your sister?" It was the opening she'd hoped for. In her research, all mention of his sister Sophie Ashman had stopped three years ago, less than six months after Crew's grandfather died from complications of pneumonia.

"Never mind," he said, stiffness entering his voice.

An awkward silence fell between them, and then he said, "Would you like to stay in here or would you be more comfortable in the living room?"

"Here's better." Tara drew out her laptop and went to the middle island, sliding onto a stool. "If you could log me into your Internet and Facebook, I could start while you're changing. I can even give myself permissions to manage the account, if that's okay."

"Sure, go to town." He typed in one password and then the other, his arm brushing hers. He smelled like dust and green meadows and sweat, which should have been a turnoff but strangely wasn't. "I didn't actually set up the account," he said, "so I'm not familiar with it except for posting."

Having researched the page and his personal profile, she

already knew that. Both had been created ten years ago, but he hadn't posted on his personal page for four years, and only a few times a year before that. "That's okay. As long as the password works."

The page came up, showing his personal profile picture. "You look about twenty there," she said with a laugh.

"I probably was." Still the tight sadness in his voice. He wandered to the edge of the kitchen before pausing to say. "Help yourself to a drink, if you want. It's in the fridge."

"Thanks."

She didn't waste any time after he disappeared. The page for the ranch was called *Silver A Thoroughbreds* and had been updated regularly before three years ago. Now that she was logged in as Crew, she saw that most of the posts had been created by Sophie Ashman and without exception, they were all about horses. No mention of the cattle side of the business at all, which according to Crew, was his focus. Obviously, his sister had lived and breathed for horses, and she'd managed the page. Tara's curiosity was killing her. Being a child who was first abandoned and then orphaned, the idea of a sibling fascinated her. The only girls she was really close to, including her roommate, were from Lily's House.

She hummed to herself as she scheduled the posts she'd created using some of the foal pictures and random facts about horses. Since it was all prepared, it was only a matter of uploading images and copying text. She'd also prepared posts about different beef cuts, recipes, and a few random pictures of calves and cattle, but those really needed to be on a different page, dedicated solely to the cattle business. All of her posts, both for the horses and cattle, were general, because there was too much she didn't know to be more specific, but she was hoping talking to Crew would shed insight about her focus.

She quickly scheduled a week of posts and created a new unpublished page entitled *Silver A Ranch* for the cattle side of the business. Feeling a sense of accomplishment, she stood and went to the refrigerator. She was used to her own jam-packed refrigerator, so this felt sparse, with only a jug of milk and several dozen varieties of bottled drinks.

She passed over the beer and grabbed a soft drink, popping it open on her way back to the counter. Did she have time to do more research before he returned? She'd already found several articles about High Vista taking over a sizeable tract of Ashman land three years ago, about the time of Sophie's disappearance. High Vista had also gained some of Silver A's Thoroughbreds, including Jump Start, in an undisclosed deal. Rumors placed Jump Start's value in the area of five million dollars, but there was no official purchase recorded. What had never been answered was why the land or the horses had changed hands. Had the Silver A been hurting for funds?

Sophie Ashman, she typed into the search of Crews friend list. Nothing. A search of Facebook brought up dozens. She didn't even know what the girl looked like or how old she was. There had been a couple of old posts on Crew's personal page with shared photos that were now listed as no content. Could those have been of Sophie and she'd removed them or taken down her page?

A sound distracted Tara, and she hurriedly cleared the search before looking up. Crew was coming toward her, looking clean and handsome. His head was hatless for a change, and she saw that his hair was indeed dark, now brushed back and glistening with water, curling slightly at the ends. He also looked freshly shaven, which surprised her because he'd been faster than she'd anticipated. The fact that he was barefooted seemed intimate.

"So, what's the verdict?" he asked.

She grinned. "I created a new page I'd like you to approve. We need to separate the focus with different pages, I think. One for the horses and one for the beef."

"Is that really necessary?" He took the stool beside her. He smelled heavenly, and it was all she could do not to lean over and sniff him. What was coming over her?

"Yes. I know you're more interested in the beef side of things, but don't you have boarding openings? Or any breeding slots?"

"Not breeding slots," he said. "I don't force my stallion like many breeders. We stick the mares in the pasture with him. It generates less income, but I feel it's more humane. He's happy as pie in the middle of his harem."

"I bet."

"But I do have stalls open, and we could add more training."

"Well then. I'll take a few pictures and see what I can do about publishing that."

"I'd be willing to pay for some ads, if you can help with them," he said.

This surprised her. But then, he'd been in business long enough to know you had to advertise to find customers.

"I don't need it for the beef, though," he added.

"So everyone knows you don't add hormones to your beef?" she asked. "I'm guessing they don't, and from what

I read, that's really big these days. And look, let me show you something." She typed in *Silver A Ranch* in the search and the first thing that came up was a three-year-old article reporting that the Silver A had lost over two hundred head of pregnant heifers to a virus, for an estimated loss of over three hundred thousand dollars. After that, the only thing listed about the ranch on the front page were mentions of Iron Express's offspring. Only on the second page did it get to hormone-free beef.

"This is what comes up first when you search for your ranch. I think getting something else there would be good for your sales, especially for your local customers or potential local customers."

He studied the article, a furrow between his eyes. "That makes sense."

"What happened to the cows?" she asked. "Does it happen a lot in raising cattle?"

He sighed. "Not on that scale. We screen new cows very carefully. That day one of the workers was careless and introduced an infected cow and then didn't report the sickness until it was too late. We were lucky that was all we lost."

"That's awful," she said. "I hope you fired him."

His expression didn't change. "He actually died in a car accident a few weeks after."

"Oh, poor man."

Crew shrugged. "It is what it is."

"And the ranch?"

"We've recovered. Or mostly. As long as nothing unforeseen happens this year, we won't have to sell off land or let men go."

"Then it would be nice to fill those stables and raise demand for Silver A beef."

A smile tugged at his mouth, which was what she'd intended. "Has anyone ever told you you're stubborn?"

"Everybody," she said with a laugh.

"I like stubborn girls."

"Are you flirting with me?"

"That depends. Do you want me to?"

Oh, did she want him to. But she just gave him what she hoped was an enigmatic grin.

"Okay," he said, "you have a budget of five hundred bucks this month between both the beef and the horses. If I see any difference, I'll continue both types of ads."

It wasn't a bad start. She could get something going for that much, though it would be better after several months. "Deal. You'll see a difference."

"You really do like a challenge."

So he did remember what she'd said yesterday. The air between them seemed to crackle, and their hands, next to each other on the counter, were suddenly too close for her comfort. She didn't know him well enough to understand what kind of a man he was, and trusting him was out of the question. Wasn't it?

"Tell me about the ranch," she said, wanting to know everything about him.

He stood and removed a beer from the refrigerator. "Why don't we go find a couch?"

She'd rather stay here where she could use the computer to put space between them. "First, let me show you the posts. And is it okay if I post the picture I took of you? Bringing a human face to the ranch will help a lot."

"That used to be my grandfather."

There was so much warmth in the words that she had to say, "You miss him."

"Yeah, I do." He settled again on the stool next to her. "He was the strong type. After my grandmother died, he held the family together."

"Your parents?"

"Around, but not really involved. My grandfather was a great man, but my father acted like a typical privileged brat—money was more important to him. And my mother . . . they didn't get along. He was jealous and she drank a lot. They ended up divorcing. I stayed here with my dad and my grandparents. Well, that was years before we built this house."

Questions threatened to come spilling out, but with effort, she bit her tongue. She didn't want the awkwardness to return. For now, she'd have to stem her curiosity about his family.

"Okay, well, here they are." She clicked into her file and began displaying the posts.

He laughed at the thought bubbles she'd put on the Thoroughbred foals. "You're funny."

"Not really. But people like funny posts."

She continued to flip through the posts as he talked about what he loved about the ranch: the quiet mornings, the first steps of a wobbly calf, riding his horse over the fields. "And most of all dinner at Isaac's," he said with a laugh.

"That explains how empty your refrigerator is."

"Yep. So what about you?" He swiveled in his chair, his knee coming into contact with her bare leg.

"Hey, we're talking about the ranch."

"No, now were talking about you." His smile ignited a flutter in her stomach. "What's your story?"

She might as well get this over with. "It's not a long one. I lost my parents early, and I grew up in foster homes. Now I work for a marketing firm."

He reached out and took her hand, his thumb rubbing over the palm. "That's your connection to Lily's House. I knew there was something."

What she knew was that he was driving her insane with his touch, but she couldn't pull away. "Lily's House was one of them. The last one—the best one."

For a long moment he didn't say anything, just kept touching her hand. Then he said quietly, "You said the girls came from neglectful or abusive situations. Which were you?"

All at once, her throat felt dry. Now who was making things awkward? Yet she didn't feel he was intruding but rather as if he cared.

At her hesitation, he added, "I'm sorry. That was rather personal. You don't have to answer if you'd rather not."

"Maybe I'm the exception—sort of. My parents weren't married when I was born, and my dad was an eighteen-year-old screw up who left us to join the army. He was killed in Afghanistan. My mother ran off with the neighbor when I was four. I went to live with my grandmother, my dad's mom. She did her best."

He sat up, his eyes suddenly intense. "Your mother left and never came back?"

Should she tell him the rest? The compassion in his eyes—would it turn to pity? "That's right. She left, and my grandmother died when I was six. After that, I went to a series of foster homes while they searched for my mother. They finally found that she'd died, but by then I was thirteen, with a chip on my shoulder. When I landed at Lily's House a year later, I hit the jackpot. I owe Lily pretty much everything. She pushed me to be better, get an education, find a good job. Now I give back." She wanted other girls to have something to hold onto like she'd found.

His thumb continued in the circle that sent delicious warmth zipping through her veins. "I can't imagine what life was like for you. We had our difficult times, but my grandfather was there, and even after my grandmother died when I was fourteen, we had Isaac's wife. She was like a second mother."

For a moment, she felt a searing jealousy that he'd had family who'd taken care of him. He'd had everything she hadn't growing up, despite his difficulties with the ranch. He'd never known hunger, had never hidden in a closet to escape abusive foster siblings, had never known what it was like to cry for a mother who had abandoned you. But she was used to that emotion, and she pushed it aside. She had so much now. She didn't need anything more.

Not even him. Though she wouldn't mind getting to know him a bit better.

His hand tightened on hers, and his face closed the space between them. Was he going to try to kiss her? It was too soon, and yet a part of her felt he'd waited far too long. She'd wanted to kiss him from the moment they'd visited the foals.

He swallowed hard and stepped away. "Would you like some ice cream? Because I have some decadent double chocolate fudge." The way he said it felt like a touch running up her back.

She laughed. "I love ice cream. Especially decadent double chocolate fudge." She'd never had it before, but it was her new favorite.

"Good." He leaned close again and said, "Because I really need to cool down right now. And for the record, yes, I'm flirting with you."

She laughed as he stepped away and pulled out two bowls from a cupboard.

He was about to pull out the ice cream when a pounding on the back door to the deck startled both of them. "Just a minute," he called. To Tara, he added, "This shouldn't take long." But his voice had grown weary.

He pulled open the door and the woman from earlier appeared, breathing hard, her red hair disheveled. "Since when do you lock the door? Look, Dad called. He needs our help with a calf."

"Now?"

The woman's eyes slid past him to Tara. "I didn't know you had company. But yes, now. Come on. I got the truck. It's too late for me to track down someone else. Where's your phone anyway?"

"Probably in the bathroom."

"I figured as much."

Crew turned to Tara. "Look, I don't know how long this will last. Birthing is like that. Can we finish this another night?" He sounded regretful, but the impatience of the other woman beckoned like a challenge to Tara. He already owed Tara one raincheck to show her the rest of the foals, and she didn't want another one.

"Can I come along? I've never seen a calf born before."

"You might not want to," the woman told her. "If it was going to be easy, she wouldn't need help."

Tara met her gaze. "I can handle it."

"Well, come on then." The woman motioned and stepped toward the door.

Tara looked at Crew to make sure he was okay with her coming. "Sure," he said. "But I need my boots." He sprinted across to the door leading to the garage.

The redhead stuck out her hand. "I'm Marti Kelley," she said. "Who are you?"

"Tara Levine."

"Nice to meet you." Marti sounded sincere and not at all like a jealous girlfriend. "Sorry for interrupting."

"That's okay."

"By the way, I'm Crew's cousin. Well, his second cousin, really. His mom and my dad are first cousins."

What a relief. And the fact that she felt such relief worried Tara. Here she was suddenly wanting to sniff a guy, getting all jealous because of his cousin, and now going off into the night to watch the birth of a calf.

Where would the end lead her? For once she couldn't say.

Marti's truck was as old as his green Toyota, and she bumped along the dirt road faster than even he did in emergencies. He hoped she didn't ruin a tire.

"Marti's going to be a veterinarian someday," he told Tara. Crammed together as they were in the cab, their legs touched, making him crazy. He should have kissed her when he had the chance, but she'd just told him about her family, and she'd seemed defenseless. When he kissed her, he wanted to be sure she kissed him back because she wanted to, not because she was feeling vulnerable.

But he wanted to kiss her badly, and he liked her more with each passing minute. He liked her humor, her certainty, her stubbornness. He liked the way she talked, the way she moved, and now he craved to know if kissing her was anything like he imagined.

Instead, they were on their way to see a calf born. Hopefully it would be healthy, despite the complications.

He looked over to see Tara smiling. "Worried?" he asked.

"Actually, I watched three cow births today on YouTube," Tara admitted. "Doing research for your social media."

"It's not the same thing."

"You can say that again," Marti agreed. "Look, Crew, I want to deliver the calf, okay? It'll be good for my resume."

He snorted. "You've helped with a ton of these."

Marti's lip protruded. "I know, but I've never done a breech alone. Dad will let me if you will."

"I'm all for you doing it," he said. "I'm wearing my good shirt." They all laughed together.

By the time they arrived at the cow pasture, Isaac had already isolated the cow using a portable stall. She was straining and bawling and straining some more. Dusk was quickly approaching, but several lanterns were already lit around the outside of the stall.

Isaac's weathered face broke into a grin as he saw them. Crew quickly made the introductions. "Nice to meet you," Isaac said to Tara, the skin around his eyes crinkling more as his grin widened.

Tara nodded. "You too."

"I'd offer a hand if it wasn't dirty." To Crew, Isaac added, "I had a feeling about this one. Came back after dinner, and sure 'nough, she was straining something awful."

"Well, let's help her out."

"Take her head, then. Marti and me'll do the rest, seeing as you have company."

Crew inclined his head in thanks. Having his arm shoulder-deep inside the backend of a cow wasn't exactly an image he wanted Tara to have as an early impression of him. "I told Marti I was fine with her pulling the calf, if that's okay with you."

Isaac grinned at his daughter. "Sure. 'Bout time for that."

They went to work. Crew thought Tara would be full of questions, but she was quiet as she watched, except for asking if she could take pictures. She snapped photos as Marti donned long plastic gloves and sank her hand inside the cow, searching for tiny hooves.

Isaac rolled his eyes and whispered loudly to Tara. "I ain't never used gloves before. Let's see if she can do it."

"Shut up, Dad." Marti grinned to show she wasn't upset. She didn't need any help finding the little hooves, pulling them out nearly a foot, and securing the rope around them.

"That doesn't hurt the baby?" Tara asked.

"No, we're careful," Isaac said.

At that moment, the cow jerked and lumbered backwards, pulling away from Crew at her head and nearly trampling Marti, who jumped out of the way.

Crew motioned to Tara to come closer and tossed her one of the ropes he was holding. "Wrap it around that lower bar there and pull it tight as Isaac pushes her forward." She watched him do it with his rope and then did the same. "Now tie it off like this, with a loop, so we can undo it quickly if we need to."

Heifer secure, Tara ventured back to the other side to watch, while Crew stayed and talked quietly to the cow. Marti began to pull with the contractions. Slowly, inch by inch, she pulled the calf out while Isaac hovered nearby, a proud smile on his face.

"It's a boy. Grab some gloves and come help!" Marti called to Tara, as she went madly to work, rubbing down the calf. "He's not breathing yet, either, so we need to get his lungs clear."

Tara didn't hesitate to drag on the gloves.

"Rub your thumbs down his nose like this," Marti told her. "And the flat of your hand under his jaw."

"I see. Like this?"

"Yes."

Tara laughed as the calf took a breath that didn't sound waterlogged. "That was incredible," she murmured.

"I know, right?" Marti's eyes were glowing with her accomplishment.

"Thank you for letting me help." Tara looked up at Crew, grinning at him as she removed her gloves. He was surprised that none of this seemed to faze her.

Finally, Crew freed the cow and they all backed away into the darkness to see what she would do next. Crew purposefully angled Tara away from the others so they could talk alone. After mooing several times, the cow turned and went to her offspring and began licking him.

"I'm glad she likes him." This Tara said almost fiercely.

Crew took her hand, and she didn't pull away. "They almost always do. They'll protect them quite loudly, in fact."

They watched the cow for a moment. "She acts like nothing happened," Tara said. "Like it was just another day."

"For a breech, this was on the easier side."

"Crazy. I thought she was going to rip in two. Marti was impressive."

He nodded. "It's in her blood. Her grandfather worked for my grandfather and on down the line."

"So is that how your parents met? Marti told me Isaac is your mom's cousin."

A knot formed in his stomach, but she had had told him

her history, and he wanted to be just as honest. "Yep, my mother hated the ranch, but she thought marrying my dad, who was going to inherit part of the ranch, was the way to big money and freedom."

"So where are your parents now?"

He hesitated, feeling the strength of her smaller hand in his. "My mother, I don't know. She was in and out for most of my early years. My grandparents raised me. After my grandmother died, my mother would be gone for a year at a time. Then one time she never came back."

"I'm sorry."

"Don't be. Like I said, she wasn't really a mother."

"And your dad?"

How much to tell her? "He was around, but not really involved." Crew was relieved when Marti joined them, cutting short the conversation.

"Hey, if you're wanting a ride home, let's go, I've got school tomorrow."

Bidding farewell to Isaac, they headed back to the truck. Marti flew down the road with even more abandon than she'd shone earlier, but Crew didn't mind as more than once Tara bumped into him, and he had to put his arm around her to steady her. The way Marti threw a grin at Crew suggested the bumping around wasn't all by accident.

When they reached the road near the back of his house and Tara had slid from the cab, Marti leaned over and whispered, "I like her."

"Me too. Just trying to have more fun like the doctor ordered. Even if my doctor is a vet."

Marti laughed. "Good." She zoomed off down the path as soon as he cleared the door.

"So," Tara said as they walked back to his house. "What now?"

"Now? We go wash our hands, and then we have some double chocolate fudge ice cream waiting for us."

"I like the sound of that."

They got into a tiny bit of a water fight in his bathroom while they washed up, which resulted in damp shirts and a lot of laughter. Then Crew scooped huge bowls of ice cream, stuck two macaroon cookies inside each, and set one on the counter in front of her.

"Everything is better with coconut," he said. "Even double chocolate fudge ice cream."

She laughed and bit into one of the cookies. "I absolutely agree."

"Well, you've seen a little of my life here," he said settling on a stool beside her. "What about you. Do you like advertising?"

"I love it." Her face lit up. "I like putting ideas together. And I like being able to work anywhere. I hope to do a little traveling someday."

"Where to?"

"Venice maybe? France? I don't really care. I just want to see a few places."

"Not to live there?"

She shook her head. "I like Phoenix." She spooned up a tiny bit of ice cream, and the way she licked it off the spoon with the tip of her tongue fascinated him.

"Me too."

A comfortable silence fell between them as they ate their ice cream.

"I do have a question," she said.

He hoped it wasn't about his father. "Yeah?"

"If you're a cattle family, how did you get into Thoroughbreds?"

"Because of my grandfather. My grandmother always loved them and she had money from her parents, but she never did anything with it. So a few years after she died, he went and bought Iron Express. That was before the horse had won anything, of course. He was just a colt, barely weaned. My grandfather hired a trainer and jockey, and we went to work."

"You liked it. I can tell."

"I loved everything about Iron Express. Still do. He's always been my horse, even though I was too heavy to race him myself. When he started winning, it surprised all of us. After that, we got a few more horses and some of them won too. They're costly to maintain, though, so eventually, my grandfather built the training stables and this house. We retired Iron Express and another horse so we could sell their breeding services. Then on my twenty-first birthday, my grandfather had a cancer scare and deeded the horse to me."

For a moment, he was tempted tell to her about Sophie and Jump Start, but a hard knot in his chest refused to comply. "I'll take you to see him sometime, if you like."

"I'd love that."

They continued to chat about the ranch and marketing, and even though Crew had to get up early, he didn't want the night to end. Finally, she scooped up the last bit of her ice cream and sighed. "I'd better start back. I'm not much of a morning person, I confess, but my boss likes me to be in at eight sharp."

"I have to be up at five."

She groaned. "Good luck with that."

He chuckled. "You get used to it. Come on, I'll walk you out. You are mostly dry, aren't you? Shouldn't be too cold even if you aren't."

"I'm pretty much dry."

They walked down the path to the parking lot. Tara stared into the sky. "It's so beautiful here. The stars are much brighter than at my apartment."

Crew looked up. "They're always this bright here, at least on clear days."

All too soon they had reached her car. They'd been together hours, but it wasn't enough for him. "So," he said, "would you like to go out with me tomorrow night?"

"I would. Where?"

He had no idea, but he wanted to impress her. "How about I surprise you? But come hungry." Dinner was a given.

"What should I wear?"

"Casual." He hoped.

"Jeans and T-shirt casual or jeans and blouse casual?"

"Blouse."

"Okay. Blouse it is."

In a second, if he didn't move, she'd be inside that car and driving away. He put his hand on her arm, and she looked up at him. "Good night."

"Good night," she repeated.

He bent over, watching her face as he closed the space between him. She leaned forward, meeting him partway. His lips met hers softly, touching once, twice, and then pulling slightly away, still close, but not touching. Their eyes held and neither drew away. That was a yes if he ever saw one. He slipped his arms around her, gently caressing her back, pulling her closer. Her arms went up around his neck. He pressed his lips to hers again more firmly, closing his eyes, breathing her in, reveling in the sensation of holding her in his arms.

Easy, boy, he told himself. He ended the kiss while he still could and stepped back. "Tomorrow at seven?"

"Perfect." Her lips looked moist and he was tempted to try it again. But she was already opening the car door.

He shut it after her and remained in the parking lot, watching her drive away.

A perfect end to the day. He could still feel her touch on his lips and smell her scent. There was only one problem.

Where was he going to take her tomorrow?

He jogged back up to the house, found his phone in the bathroom, and texted Marti. *Help. I have a date tomorrow and I have no idea where to take her.*

She texted back almost immediately. *That's because you're lame and are bent on working yourself to death.*

I thought you were going to bed.

I'm too wound up to sleep. Okay, I got it. Take her to Kimbo's for dinner and dancing.

Dancing? I haven't been in years.

So what? Big baby. If you're lucky, I'll stop by and introduce you to the man I'm going to marry.

I don't want you horning in on my date. He was rethinking this whole asking for her help idea.

Too bad. Take her flowers. You are picking her up, right?

Of course. What kind of flowers?

What kind does she like?

No idea.

Then take your favorite kind.
He sighed. *Thanks.*
Did you kiss her?
None of your business.
Ha! You did! Good job. See you tomorrow night.

Rylee looked her over critically, one finger tapping her bottom lip. "Yep, I think you'll do."

Tara stared down at her blue skinny jeans and high heels. "Are you sure the heels aren't too fancy? He did say casual."

"Maybe. But he's tall enough, right? Where are your black ones?"

Tara knew exactly where they were—back in Crew's office. She'd forgotten all about them. "I left them somewhere," she admitted. "So they're not an option."

"They wouldn't match as well as these pink ones anyway. Besides, if anything isn't casual, it's that blouse."

Tara touched the gauzy ruffles on her dusty pink blouse. Tiny silver sequins were set at intervals and maybe it was a little fancy, though the shirt had been less than fifteen bucks at a retail discount store. They matched her heels perfectly. "You think it's too much?"

"Who cares? You look fabulous, and he did say blouse."

Tara smiled at her roommate gratefully. "Thanks, I needed that."

Rylee tilted her head, her blond locks swaying outward. "You really like this guy, don't you?"

"I do." Tara took the few steps to their couch and sat down. "You know how it is when you first kiss someone and you're trying to get it right? You're moving around and back and forth a bit, trying to find a good position. Well, it wasn't like that. It was perfect. We just knew how we fit. And what a kiss!" She'd been up half the night thinking about it.

Rylee made a face. "At least one of us is getting some meaningful kisses. I swear, something's wrong with most men I meet. They don't want a relationship, they just want to make out—or more. I'd like to at least know I'm going to see them again before I get to that point."

"They're blind, is what," Tara told her. Rylee was model gorgeous with a slender figure, great hair, and smooth skin. While Tara was always trying to drop a few pounds, Rylee had the metabolism of an athlete, never mind that she hated to exercise. She worked at a mortgage firm and was well on her way up the corporate ladder. She was also fun to be around.

The doorbell rang, but before Tara could rise, Rylee sat down next to her and took her hand. "Look, you give him a chance. Really get to know him. Trust your heart."

"But—"

"No, you know what I'm talking about. You always give up too soon. Like with Steven from downstairs, or Dennis, that guy Lily set you up with."

Tara's protest died on her lips. Steven was an owner of two restaurant franchises and a really nice guy, and Dennis, a pilot, had made her laugh. Both had seemed to really like her. But she'd broken it off with both after only three dates because neither had seen their families in two years.

They had families and discarded them, while she, who never had a family of her own, clung to the one Lily had given her. Men like that didn't commit or stick around, in her opinion, and she saw the "ending" with each man as them walking away. At least that was what her gut said. Better not to risk her heart. Now Steven was married and Dennis was engaged. Tara didn't know if that meant her "ending" sensor was off or that they'd found women who'd changed things for them.

The doorbell rang again. Tara pulled her hand away. "Of course I'm giving him a chance. I kissed him, didn't I?"

Tara bounced up from the couch and hurried to the door, sweeping up her house key on her way and putting it into her pocket next to a few bills. She'd thought about taking a purse, but she didn't want to be stuck carrying it all night.

"Hey, bring him in so I can meet him. I don't want to hover." Rylee gave her an eager smile.

"Fine." Tara opened the door, and her breath caught in her throat. Crew stood there, looking striking in black jeans, a white western shirt, and a black cowboy hat. In his hands, he held a vase of beautiful wild flowers.

His eyes gleamed and his smile widened. "You look amazing."

"Thank you. So do you." She was glad for the blouse and high heels now.

He handed her the flowers, and her hands barely fit around the bottom of the vase. "These are beautiful," she said. They reminded her of spring, of camping with the girls from Lily's House, of morning and sunshine.

"I didn't know your favorite kind. These are mine."

"They're perfect." No one had ever given her wild flowers before. "Come on in while I put these inside."

He followed her into the apartment. "This is my roommate, Rylee," she said. "Rylee, this is Crew."

Rylee arose from the couch and came toward them. "Nice to meet you."

Tara could tell from her voice that she was impressed. Crew was probably just as impressed. Men usually loved looking at Rylee. In fact, she was starting to wish she hadn't invited him inside or introduced them.

That's silly, she thought. Rylee was her best friend and had been since they'd met at Lily's House ten years ago. She wasn't going to make a play for Crew.

"Nice to meet you," Crew said, offering his hand.

Rylee smiled as she shook. "I didn't expect a cowboy."

Tara hoped she wouldn't say anything about how she normally avoided any guy with boots or a hat. She filled the vase with water and set it on the counter, then hurried back to Crew, who wasn't staring at Rylee, but watching her instead. A breathless feeling started in her chest, the same feeling she had right before he kissed her last night.

"Bye Rylee," she said, waving at her roommate.

"Have fun." Rylee gave her a smirk. "I won't wait up."

Crew's silver truck awaited them downstairs. "Ah, good to see I merit the nice truck."

He opened the door for her. "Only the best for you."

The truck was rather large, and he offered a hand to help her inside, and though she didn't need it, she accepted his offer.

"Where are we going?" she asked, once he'd started the engine.

"Kimbo's. You ever been there?"

"No. Never heard of it."

"Then you're in for a surprise." He started the engine. "Uh, I think I should probably warn you that Marti and her boyfriend might be stalking us tonight."

She laughed. "Really?"

"Yeah, I think she wants to make sure I don't scare you away."

"You're not scary." But he was. Really scary. Because her heart was working overtime just being close to him, and she wanted more than anything to scoot over and snuggle with him as he drove.

"But I don't mind," she added. "Marti's nice." It might be easier having someone around in case they ran out of things to say.

Kimbo's turned out to be a dinner and dancing place, and most everyone wore western attire, including boots and cowboy hats. But enough of the women wore high heels, so Tara didn't feel out of place. For all their height, these high heels were the most comfortable she owned after the black ones.

"How's the calf?" she remembered to ask as they were led to a table that was one of several dozen bordering a huge dance floor.

"Doing great. And eleven more were born today, all without help. The numbers should go up from here on out until all of them are born."

Tara scarcely noticed what they ordered because he was telling her about how calves were normally birthed earlier in the year and sold in the fall, and how he hoped a summer crop would lead to larger profits the next year.

She was fascinated with the concept of switching things up, and it gave her ideas for more social media posts. She'd already scheduled two weeks out on both Facebook pages, designed one ad, started two twitter accounts, an Instagram, a Google+, and a Pinterest. It was a simple matter of resizing and posting the same images, so it wasn't that much more effort.

"So enough about me," he said, as the waiter brought their steaks. "Tell me about what you do at work."

"Well, I do all aspects of digital marketing, including optimizing websites for conversion. I do a lot with SEO, which is basically dealing with posts and key words. I also design ads." She took a bite of her meat. "Wow, this is great."

He grinned. "It's from the Silver A."

"And they just happened to carry your beef?"

"Actually, I used to come here a lot and the steak was awful, so I went to see the owner."

"Good initiative. I wonder if he'll give us an endorsement for your website. That's one thing I noticed you didn't have."

They talked on about her job and the ranch and how Kate and Brin were doing with their new assignments. When Marti showed up with her boyfriend, there hadn't been one lull in the conversation, and Tara regretted their appearance.

"Hi guys. Sorry we're late," Marti said. "This is Trevor Hadfield. Trevor, this is my cousin Crew and his date, Tara . . ."

"Levine," Tara supplied. "Nice to meet you." Crew stood to shake hands with Trevor before they both sat down.

Marti and Trevor wore plaid shirts and cowboy boots,

and Trevor wore a brown cowboy hat over his blond hair. "We already ate at Trevor's parents' house," she said, stealing a french fry from Crew's plate, "but I'll have one of these."

"She'll do anything for fries," Trevor said.

Marti stole another one. "Crew's finished anyway. They always give too many here." Everyone laughed, and the next minute they were talking about food and school and Trevor's family.

"Oh good," Marti said after ten minutes, "the dancing is starting. Let's go." She bounced to her feet, grabbing Trevor's hand and pulling him up. "Be warned, Tara, Crew takes his country dancing seriously." Laughing, she pulled Trevor to the dance floor.

Crew set down his drink. "Would you like to dance?"

"Sure." Butterflies were tickling her stomach. Dancing was something Tara enjoyed and was good at, but she hoped the country moves wouldn't be too different from what she knew.

Almost from the first steps, her worry vanished. Crew was a good dancer and a great leader. There was a bit of a learning curve, but Crew was patient, showing her the steps during the line dancing. But most of the steps were familiar and soon Tara was laughing and dancing, flushed and hot every bit as much as from his touch as from the exertion. They were in sync. At one point, Crew removed his hat and left it on their table.

Finally, he pulled her to him in a two-step slow dance. He leaned over and whispered in her ear. "Do you know how much I want to kiss you right now?"

Her heart slammed into high gear. She whispered back. "Only if it's as much as I want to kiss you."

His chuckle sent a shiver up her back. She was lost in his arms, falling, falling, with no desire of being caught. There was so much she didn't yet know about him, but being here was right.

He kissed her cheek near her ear, and the anticipation made her want to kiss him even more.

Then the music changed to a faster dance. "Later," he said, as a promise.

They continued dancing, but only a minute into the new number, Crew stopped and stood still, the color fading from his face as he stared at something behind her. "What . . .?" she turned and saw a slender, petite girl, whose back was toward them. She had long blond hair to her waist and wore a black tank top, jean shorts, and blue cowboy boots.

"Sophie!" Crew strode toward her, placed a hand on her shoulder.

The girl turned. She was young—probably still in her teens. "Hi, do you need something?"

Crew dropped his hand. "Sorry, I thought you were someone else." He turned back to Tara, his face still sickly pale under his tan.

"Are you okay?" she asked.

"Yeah, fine." But his voice was stiff and his eyes sad. "Do you mind if we take a little break?"

"Sure, I could use one."

"I'll meet you back at the table." He strode off in the direction of the men's room, while Tara stared after him.

When he'd disappeared, she wandered back to the table, where Marti was sitting alone. "Where's Crew?" she asked over the music.

"Pit stop, I think."

Marti wasn't fooled. "What happened?"

Tara was torn between wanting to understand and not wanting to betray Crew. But he hadn't asked her not to say anything. "He thought he saw Sophie. She has blond hair, right?"

"You haven't seen a picture?" Marti brought out her phone and flipped through her photo album until she found what she was looking for. "Here she is. Of course, this was three years ago. She was twenty-one."

Tara took the phone and immediately saw why Crew had made the mistake. Sophie had a mass of blond hair and was short just like the girl on the dance floor. In this picture, she was also wearing very short shorts and cowboy boots.

"The girl looked just like her. Well, except for the face." Tara handed back the phone.

"I bet he was upset."

To put it mildly. "Maybe he won't come back." Good thing she had brought her phone and her emergency money. The thought made her chest hurt.

"Of course he'll be back." Marti frowned at her. "Crew always comes back. He's as solid as everyone else in his family is flakey. Well, I mean his immediate family, because his grandparents on his dad's side were great, and those of us in his mom's family don't have any issues. Just her."

The tension seeped from Tara. "So what happened to her? Sophie, I mean, not his mom."

"He didn't tell you?"

Tara started to say that they'd only met two days ago, but that really wasn't the reason he hadn't told her. They'd talked about everything else, including how she'd landed at Lily's House and about his mother leaving and his cattle dying. "I don't think he likes to talk about her."

"Sounds like him." Marti looked around the dance floor, as if searching for Crew. "Well, Sophie ran away because she was supposed to receive the deed to a horse named Jump Start on her twenty-first birthday, but it didn't work out that way. Their grandfather died before she turned twenty-one, and in his will, their father received specific land that had once belonged to Crew's grandmother and also a percentage of the Thoroughbreds. He took Jump Start and some of the other better horses and went into a partnership with a guy who was opening another breeding farm. He'd always wanted to grow that part of the business, and he knew Crew would never agree."

"Let me guess—High Vista?" Tara was beginning to understand why Crew had been upset when he thought she worked for the company.

"Yes, them. Crew's father basically gave High Vista the land and the horses in the partnership. Never mind that everyone knew Jump Start was meant for Sophie. Those two were inseparable, at least once Jump Start wasn't racing anymore. The only reason Iron Express didn't end up there as well is because he already belonged to Crew."

"Why didn't their grandfather leave Jump Start to Sophie?"

"Well, that was the plan, but Sophie was a little wild at seventeen when he deeded Iron Express over to Crew, so he decided to wait until Sophie was older. Then he died before he could make sure she got the horse. Legally, there was nothing we could do about it."

"It broke her heart."

"Yes, and all of our hearts right along with her." Marti sighed. "I wasn't there the day she left, but there was a huge fight. Sophie had learned long ago not to trust her father, but she blamed Crew for not stopping him. He blamed himself too. Still does."

"I take it Crew and his father aren't on good terms." No wonder the man had never come up in their conversations except briefly.

Marti shrugged. "Well, he died in a car crash right after. So we'll never know what might have happened."

Died? No wonder Crew didn't talk about him. "But if he's dead, wouldn't Crew and Sophie get back his share of High Vista?"

"I wish. Everything in the partnership went to the survivor, so High Vista walked off with the land and horses without a single payment. Or rather, they keep it as long as they fulfill the terms of the contract, which I'm not really sure about. Something about staying in business a certain number of years. They seem to be doing it, though. The guy at High Vista has a rich father who's been financing a lot of their costs."

That would explain all the marketing dollars.

"To make matters worse," Marti continued, "Crew's father introduced some sick heifers into our herd, and we lost two hundred pregnant cows."

"That was him?" Tara felt sick. But it made sense since only someone with authority would purchase new cattle, and Isaac was obviously too experienced to make that sort of blunder. Plus, Crew had said the man responsible died in a car accident.

"Yep." Again Marti looked around, as if to make sure

Crew couldn't hear them. "It's been a struggle ever since, but Crew, he didn't take the easy way out and let the help go. He just got a loan and kept going. I think he hoped his father would come around, but then he died."

"That's horrible."

She nodded. "It was a bad time."

"Maybe I should go find him."

"He'll be back. Give him a little time."

Frustration welled up inside Tara. Having Crew disappear like that called up all kinds of insecurities in her that she wasn't proud of. Just when things were going so well. "Does he always get upset if you mention Sophie?"

Marti nodded. "I think it's because he doesn't know what happened to her, or if she's even okay. He went to the police at the time, and they basically came back and told him she was fine and didn't want to see him. They told him they'd grant her a restraining order if he didn't lay off. The two of them had been so close, and he didn't understand how she could do that. I still don't understand it myself." Marti fell silent as Trevor returned with two drinks.

"Can I get you something?" he asked Tara.

"No, thank you." Tara rose to her feet. "I think I'll go to the little girls' room, though." If Crew hadn't come back by the time she returned, she'd text him that she was leaving. What else could she do? Maybe he needed to be alone.

She'd taken only a few steps away from the table when an arm slipped around her, and she turned to see Crew.

"Where're you going?" he said in her ear.

"The bathroom."

He grinned. "Be warned. There's a line. That's why I

took so long. But I'll get us a drink while you're gone. Any requests?"

Relief made her throat tight. He'd come back like Marti had promised. "Surprise me." She started to walk away, but his hand tightened slightly over hers, tugging her back. She turned and met his eyes.

"Sorry about that back there. She looked like my sister."

"I figured that much out. You don't know where she is?"

"No." He leaned over and kissed her cheek. "It doesn't matter. I was just surprised."

Tara wanted to tell him she knew about Jump Start and what his father had done, but she didn't think it would help anything. She most certainly wasn't going to tell him she'd thought he'd dumped her tonight. Instead, she hugged him.

He gave the softest of sighs as he returned her embrace. People jostled past them and the music boomed, but she didn't care.

He released her, grinning. "Hurry up. We need to dance more."

"Okay." Strange how fast she could go from worried and upset to flying high with the anticipation of being close to him.

In the bathroom, she stared at herself in the mirror. Her cheeks were flushed and her smile wide. Her eyes looked happy. *I really like him,* she admitted to the face in the mirror.

By the time she got back to the table, she was feeling anxious again, but the others were laughing about something, and there was no sign of Crew's distress. Tara gave herself up to the moment, sitting next to him, with his arm curled around her until they finished their drinks. Then they danced until her feet hurt.

"Tired?" Crew asked.

"Hey, you're the one who has to get up at five." She took out her phone. "It's almost midnight."

"Don't worry about me. I'm used to it."

But they told Marti and Trevor goodbye and left. "Finally, I have you to myself," Crew said, as they walked to his truck.

Tara's stomach was fluttery again, and the feeling grew as he drove to her apartment and walked her inside the complex and up the stairs to her door. She didn't move to take out her key. "That was fun."

"It was." His voice was low and slightly rough. "Tara?"

"Yes?"

"I think I'm going to kiss you."

"I'm okay with that."

They started kissing, and she melted into him, giving herself up to the moment. When he drew away, he was smiling. "Can I see you tomorrow? How about that horse-back ride we talked about?"

Yes! she wanted to shout. "Don't you have to work?" She knew enough to understand that Saturday was like any other day at the ranch for him.

"I can get away." His grin widened. "Or I'll show you a little of what I do. You can help."

That made her laugh. "Okay."

He waited until she opened her door and then kissed her again, long and slowly. Something inside her clicked, like a switch turning on. She wanted the moment to go on forever, and yet somehow the promise of tomorrow was enough. He drew reluctantly away, and with a smile, headed back down the stairs.

Tara shut the door softly and sighed. Could this really be happening to her? She sank down on the couch and whispered, "I think I'm falling for him." The thought was terrifying and exciting all at once. Terrifying because of the power he would have over her, and exciting because of the power they could create together.

Only one thing marred her happiness, and that was Crew's reaction to questions about his sister. Would Sophie's abandonment continue to be something that stood between them, or would he open up about her?

One thing for sure was that he was in pain regarding Sophie. It was a door that, for him at least, wasn't shut. And why? He needed to repair things between them or let it go. Otherwise, it could affect all his relationships. She knew because, despite all the therapy she'd undergone as a teen at Lily's House, she still had trouble trusting people because of her past. *They always leave,* she thought.

But it wasn't really true. Lily and her husband stayed, and her foster sisters were still her best friends.

The key to Crew's pain was Sophie. Where was she now? Was she ready to forgive?

Tara pulled out her phone and brought up Marti's number. She hadn't thought to use it so soon when they exchanged numbers this evening, but it felt right.

Let's find Sophie, she typed in a text.

The response was immediate. *Yes! I told him it was time, but he's too proud.*

Marti was wrong. Crew wasn't too proud. He was too wounded. Behind his determination to make the Silver A Ranch a success, there was a lot of hurt piled up in his past, and her heart ached to understand that.

I need her picture, and her full name, she sent to Marti. *And anything else you think will help.*

Right. I'll start on finding stuff the minute I get home.

The next day at ten when Tara arrived at the ranch, Crew saddled up Iron Express and Dancer, one of his favorite mares, and took Tara out onto his land. Acre after acre stretched out before them. There was no way he could show it all to her, but he could show her his main herd and a few of his favorites spots.

He was excited to see that she knew her way around a horse. "I was one of the first who worked with Tessa's horse," she told him when he asked.

"Tessa is Lily's sister, right?"

"Yeah, sorry. And she's also the psychologist for the girls. Anyway, I learned from her."

"Well, you're a natural. I'll have you roping cows in no time."

"I doubt that."

"We'll see." He leaned over and she met him halfway over their horses for a kiss. She tasted intoxicatingly of mint and warmth.

She was suitably impressed with the size of the main herd, which numbered three hundred and fifty animal units. "We've got two other herds. We run a total of seven hundred animal units on a hundred and fifty thousand acres. A thousand acres belong to the ranch. The rest we lease from the government."

"What are animal units?"

"A cow and her calf, basically." There was more to it, because each unit had a general weight limit, but that wasn't important for this explanation. "We can actually run a hundred more, but we're still recovering."

"From losing the cattle, right?"

"Right." He hesitated before adding, "About that. The man who died in the car accident after killing my cows? That was my father." He didn't want her hearing it from someone else, and after she'd told him about her parents, he wanted her to know.

Her breath caught in her throat. "Oh, Crew, I'm so sorry." She hesitated before adding, "I should tell you that Marti did mention something about it last night, but I really appreciate you telling me."

"Yeah, Marti's got a big mouth." To his surprise, his father's actions didn't hurt as much as they once had, at least not the part about the cattle. Maybe someday he'd be able to tell Tara about Jump Start and Sophie. But at the thought of his sister, a pit opened in his stomach and anger soured his gut. He pushed back the emotion. *Get over it.* He only hoped Marti hadn't spilled his other secrets as well. He'd talk to her about staying out of his business.

"Now the next place I'm taking you to is really special," he said.

"I can't wait."

He led her to what they called the upper meadow, where

wild flowers filled a small valley next to a little stream. Tiny purple, pink, red, white, and yellow flowers spread out like a colorful blanket.

"It's beautiful!" Tara dismounted and went down the incline to wade into the flowers. Crew joined her. "Your favorite flowers," she said. "You picked them here."

He was pleased she recognized them, but also a little unsure if picking them himself made them less valuable, despite the added trouble he'd gone to. He'd wanted to share them with her. "That's right. This was my grandmother's favorite place. She used to bring us here for picnics."

She hugged him. "I love that you brought me here—and that I have some of these flowers back at my apartment. Now whenever I see them, I'll remember this day."

"Good. Come see this then." Grabbing her hand, he led her across the meadow to the big tree where they'd always had their picnics. Thanks to Julie, a blanket was already spread there underneath bug-proof containers filled with food.

She laughed. "Perfect."

She was right. The nearly two hours they spent together were perfect, but all too soon it was over and he had to go back to work. "Can I come by tonight?" he asked her as they readied to leave. "It probably won't be until eight. We're moving one of the herds to a new pasture—that's pretty much a daily task around here. Frequent rotations help maintain the grass at a decent level so it grows back better."

"I'd love to see you whenever you finish. I'll pick up some double chocolate fudge ice cream and macaroons and we can watch a movie or something."

"That would be great." He kissed her and she kissed him

back, but he could tell she was distracted. "What are you thinking?"

"Just about you coming here with your grandmother. Were your sister and Marti here too?" When he nodded, she added, "It must have been nice."

He could sense the longing in her voice, and he wished so much that he could give her those memories. Of him chasing the girls through the flowers, splashing in the stream, or giving in to their demands to help them make flower crowns for their heads. Well, he couldn't change Tara's lack of happy memories, but he could help create more perfect memories, if she would let him.

On their ride back, his thoughts drifted to Sophie. Marti had urged him to do something about her, but what could he do? He'd tried to find her before and the police were no help. And he was still so angry at her . . . and at himself.

What he needed was to get Jump Start back, but the only way that would happen was if he could drive High Vista out of business, which would invalidate his father's partnership and return what he'd put into the business to his heirs.

Except that wasn't the only way. There was one more thing Crew could do to strike a bargain with High Vista, but he had resisted the temptation because he hadn't wanted to give Dervin any more benefits, or reward the way he'd taken advantage of his drunken father.

Maybe it was time he capitulated. It might be the only way to set things right.

After Tara left, Crew made the phone call to High Vista from the field where Iron Express was grazing with his mares. He couldn't help his relief that Dervin didn't pick up.

A message would give both of them more time to consider an arrangement. Crew planned to talk to Isaac, of course, before the deal was final. And maybe Marti as well.

"Hello, this is Crew Ashman. I've been thinking about your offer to buy Iron Express. I'm not interested in a sale, but I might be willing to consider a trade that includes Jumps Start. Think about it and call me when you get a chance."

He hung up, watching the stallion notice him and come galloping over. He held out a carrot. "Hey boy," he said. "I don't want to do this, but they'll take good care of you because of what you're worth."

Iron Express tossed his head and snorted, which was exactly the way Crew felt about High Vista. Well, it wasn't a done deal yet. He was only exploring his options.

Even so, a little piece of him withered as he mounted his other horse and went to work.

Tara stopped by Lily's House on the way back from the ranch, and she discovered Lily reading a romance novel on the back deck. "Missing Mario?" Tara teased. She knew Lily's husband had been at his parents' in Tucson the past two days helping them remodel their kitchen.

"Actually, yes. Plus, my kids are at my sister's, and the girls all went to the mall, so I'm reading, even though I have a thousand other things I should be doing. It's good for the soul. What's up?" Lily set her book on the little table beside her lounge chair.

Tara settled on another of the dozen chairs spread out over the deck. "I need to find somebody." She told her about Sophie and how she wanted to help Crew reunite with her.

"It sounds like you're serious about him."

"Maybe." Tara could feel the silly look on her face and was glad Lily didn't say any more. "He's told me a lot about his past, but this thing with his sister . . . I don't know. He just . . . he's not happy." There, that was the bottom line. "I think if he doesn't deal with it, then it might ruin things for us because as it is, he can't talk about her. I'm even worried he'll be upset when he finds out I'm looking for her."

"Wait, let's go back to the part where he can't talk about it yet. You've only known him for four days."

"Four *incredible* days," Tara corrected, but she knew Lily was right. She also knew she wasn't backing down.

Lily laughed. "Then shouldn't you tell him you want to help him find her?"

"No. Definitely not. He's already been through a lot. I want to feel her out before I tell him."

"Okay, so find her."

"That's just it. I *can't* find her. Last night after our date, I spent hours online and then again this morning. I've checked out dozens of Sophies on Facebook all over the country."

All versions of Sophie's name, including her mother's maiden name, Kelley, which was also her middle name, brought up a lot of people, but none of them seemed to be her. Only old statements in news articles seemed to reference the real woman. "She can't have dropped off the face of the earth."

"You have a picture?"

"Yes, and I tried an image look up on the Internet. I had no idea there were some many similar-looking people in the world. None of them are her—at least that I can tell. Now if I had access to a photograph I knew she'd posted online on some account, it would be different because the search engines could maybe find the exact one, but this picture is from his cousin, and it was never posted online."

"Didn't she have a Facebook page before all this happened?"

"Yes, but she must have blocked Crew and his cousin because all the posts from her on their personal profiles are missing."

"Were they in any groups together? Because if anyone else could see her posts, they might be able to give you the URL. Just because he's blocked doesn't mean you won't be able to see it."

"He doesn't have time for Facebook, so no groups, and I don't even think she's using her original account. On the ranch's page when I'm logged in as an admin on my own account, I can see her name as the creator of most of the posts, but clicking it just brings up a broken link icon, as if her profile has been unpublished or deleted. When I'm logged in as Crew, the link to her name is grayed out. I'm thinking she must have known even if she blocked her family, they could still find her through dummy accounts if she kept the same one."

"Well, if pictures of her don't work, what about pictures of her horse? All the ones she has of him should be older, and if she's made a new page, she'll probably post at least a couple for memory's sake, right?"

Tara stared at her. "Lily, you're a genius! I should have thought of that. I do have some with Jump Start that Marti sent me, but Sophie was so far away in them that I didn't think the search engines would recognize her face. I forgot that maybe Sophie might post the same picture. She wouldn't have any newer ones since she doesn't own Jump Start anymore."

Lily's grin widened with the compliment. "Well, it still might not work. It'd have to be the exact same picture because there are too many horses and riders who look exactly alike. At least to me."

Tara drew out her laptop from her bag. She had brought it to Crew's this morning in case they had time for her to show him a few ideas for future posts—which they hadn't— but now it felt like fate. "Well, let's just see."

Her fingers flew over the keys. She tried eleven pictures of Sophie with Jump Start without any result. But the twelfth one brought up exactly two other pictures of the same image, one posted on Facebook and the other on Pinterest. Both posts were only a few months old. Excitement flooded her. Finally, a lead. She clicked on the Facebook link.

Lily leaned closer as the profile loaded, the picture of the horse at the top of the page. On the bottom left side, the profile photo revealed a mysterious young girl looking to the side, her face half in shadow. Her hair barely reached her jaw.

"What happened to her hair?" Lily squinted at the screen as if that would change something. "I mean, that's a fabulous cut, but it totally changes her. In fact, you sure it's her?"

Tara was sure. Sophie had the same soulful brown eyes as Crew, and her smile, how it tipped up ever-so-slightly even with her serious expression, was exactly like his. "It's her, but look at the name, SKA. Sophie Kelley Ashman. It's her initials. Her mother's maiden name is her middle name. It says she's in Phoenix. If this is right and she's still here, how is it possible they haven't run into her?"

"There's over a million and a half people here," Lily said.

She had a point, especially with Crew working so hard

and Marti in school. "Let's see . . . she works at Monkey Pants Bar & Grill. That's vaguely familiar." Tara looked it up. "Oh, a bar in Tempe."

Thoughts tumbled through her mind. She could easily make it there before Crew came over tonight. Of course, she had no idea if Sophie was working. "I'm going to check out the bar," she said, standing abruptly.

Lily swung her feet off the lounge, worry wrinkling the skin around her eyes. "Are you sure about that?"

"No." But she liked Crew and she wanted to make sure Sophie wouldn't hurt him before she told him where Sophie was. If Sophie even still worked there. "But what if I find her and she's a horrible person?"

"I guess you'll have to see. But just remember to give her the benefit of the doubt. You know how some of the girls were when they arrived here."

"Me."

Lily smiled. "Yes. So don't judge."

Tara stood. "Okay, I won't."

"I still think you should tell him, though. Because he should know."

"I will eventually. Now you get back to your romance novel. I'll let you know later how it goes."

Twenty minutes and a dose of heartburn later, Tara walked into the Monkey Pants Bar & Grill. At two in the afternoon, the place wasn't hopping, but there was a lingering lunch clientele. The stage where they held a weekly comedy show was empty now. She weaved through the tables, slowly approaching the bar. There were two bartenders, both men, but the clang of dishes told her someone was in the back cooking.

She took her time surveying the place, not really wanting to order anything, especially if Sophie wasn't there. After only a few minutes, she determined that Sophie was nowhere in the bar, unless she was in the back. Tara would probably need to ask about her, but for now she'd slip into the bathroom and see if she happened to be there or if there was a waitress to ask.

Two women were in the bathroom, but neither looked like an employee. One woman, a brunette, was adjusting her low shirt so her bra wouldn't show. The other woman was blond, but she was at least ten years older than Tara's twenty-five, so definitely not Sophie. Tara exchanged smiles with them before washing her hands.

Leaving the bathroom, she rallied her courage to ask for Sophie. Otherwise, she'd have to hang out here all night and miss her date with Crew. She slid onto a barstool and ate some of the free popcorn as she waited for the bartender. There was only one there now. She craned her neck to see into the kitchen, but it was hopeless.

When the bartender reached her, Tara took a deep breath and said, "Hey, is Sophie working tonight?"

"Sorry, I'm new here. I don't know any Sophie. You a friend of hers?"

"We have mutual friends. Just thought I'd say hi."

"Well, I can go in the back and ask once I help everyone. What can I get you?"

"I think I'll come back later. See if she's here then."

"Suit yourself." He went to help another customer.

Outside in her car, Tara texted Marti. *I may have a lead on Sophie.*

Already?

Maybe. Might be old information. Tonight she'd go over Sophie's Facebook page to see if there was anything she'd missed. She'd already requested to be friends with several of Sophie's friends in the hopes of finding someone who knew her in real life.

Well, let me know, Marti responded. *It will be a miracle. I just hope Sophie wants us to find her.*

Tara hoped so too.

10

For the next few days, Tara found herself spending more time with Crew. They watched a movie, had dinner at the ranch with Marti's family, and went on another horseback ride. When they weren't together, Tara found herself working more on his social media than doing her usual unpaid overtime for her boss. Using social media, she'd filled two of Crew's open boarding slots, and two local restaurants had contracted with him for fresh beef.

"You're gloating," he said when he called her Tuesday morning at work with the news.

She smirked. "You bet I am. And you have nearly three hundred new likes on both Facebook pages. I think it's time to do a giveaway. Not only will we get more notice, but the way we'll set it up, you'll be able to add them to your existing newsletter list."

"What would I give away?"

"A training lesson, a two-hour horseback ride? A side of hormone-free beef? Stud services?" She'd mocked each of these up last night, so it was only a matter of starting the Facebook ad and publishing the giveaway page on his website. "Something that has real value for them but doesn't cost you so much that it's prohibitive."

"Prohibitive?" He laughed. "I love it when you use big words. Do it for a horseback ride and a side of beef then." His voice lowered. "Look, we're having an issue with a couple of our wells, so I have to work tonight, but can I see you tomorrow?"

"Sure. What should we do?"

"Let's cook dinner together here. I have my grand-mother's recipe for garlic chicken."

"Garlic chicken? Are you sure that's the best choice?" she teased. With all the kissing they'd be doing, she meant.

"You'll love it. I promise. And if we're *both* eating garlic . . ." His voice was like a caress, sending spicy shudders throughout her body.

"Sounds fun." Actually, it sounded a little serious, especially with the way she felt about him, and she didn't know if it was a good idea to be there alone or how far to let it go. She was falling for him hard. *They always leave,* she reminded herself. She couldn't forget that. Plus, there was Sophie and his unfinished business with her.

"Good. You don't have to worry about bringing anything. I'll pick up everything tomorrow."

"You'd better grab some frozen pizzas in case we utterly fail."

He chuckled. "It's garlic chicken, not rocket science."

"I guess we'll see about that. See you tomorrow."

After the conversation, Tara could barely concentrate on her ad campaign, so she worked through her morning break to make up the time she'd wasted. For lunch, she headed back to the Monkey Pants Bar & Grill. The place was crowded, but to her surprise, Sophie was there. What now? She had to tell Crew.

Sophie's hair was longer than the picture on Facebook, down to her shoulders, but pulled back from her face. She looked happy, and a sudden guilt attacked Tara. This had been the right thing to do, tracking Sophie, hadn't it?

Tara watched for a moment to make sure she sat at the bar where Sophie would most likely be the one to help her. Within a minute, Sophie came to take her order. "Can I get you something?"

Tara ordered the first thing on the menu without thinking. While Sophie was filling her order, she drew out her phone and turned it on, smiling at the picture of Crew's foal that she was using for her screen background. Should she tell Crew she'd found Sophie? Lily seemed to think so, and she was generally right about . . . well, about everything. But what if things exploded?

At any rate, when she did tell him, it was something that should be done in person, not through a text. Sighing, she set the phone down on the bar, smiling again at the picture of the foal.

Sophie brought her food, her eyes falling to Tara's phone. "Oh, what a gorgeous little foal. Is it yours?" Sophie appeared to drink in the picture, her smile wide.

Tara picked up the phone. What to say? Tell the truth? Distract her?

"It's supposed to be a gray," she said, handing the phone to Sophie. "I'm not clear exactly why it's not gray yet though."

"Oh, they get their gray later. Depending on their genes, some mares will always have grays and some will have gray offspring only part of the time. The foals are usually black until they start changing."

"I think this one's mother only has grays." Should she say more, tell her who it belonged to? "So you know about horses."

Sophie shrugged, her smile fading a little. "I owned a few once. Is this one a Thoroughbred? Looks like it."

"Yeah," Tara said.

Another bartender called Sophie's attention, and she handed back the phone. "Enjoy your meal. Let me know if you need anything."

There had been no more opportunity to talk before Tara had to hurry back to work, and maybe that was for the best. She'd already gone over her lunch hour and would have to work late to make up that time.

Tara headed over to Lily's House after work, wanting to tell Lily about seeing Sophie, since it was her idea that led her there. Lily was shopping, but Kate and Brin were in the kitchen making macaroons, so Tara chatted with them as she waited for Lily. Both girls looked tan and healthy.

"These are to take to everyone at the ranch tomorrow," Kate told her, popping a small ball of dough into her mouth.

Was it just in Tara's mind, or had Kate eased up slightly on the black makeup? She also looked like she'd dropped a pound or two, and she was wearing a light blue Silver A Ranch shirt, which was a decided improvement over her usual black clothing. "I like your shirt," Tara said.

"Mr. Ashman gave them to us." Kate twirled around, modeling the shirt. "But that's not the best part."

Brin laughed. "Kate has a crush on one of the stable boys."

"Not that!" Kate said. "It's Iron Express. We got to ride him today!"

"You did?" Tara was surprised.

Kate nodded. "That's right. It was an awful day, really. Cleaning out all those stalls. It sometimes gets old. I love exercising the horses, but it was beginning to feel like we'd never get to ride any of the Thoroughbreds, even though Mr. Ashman promised we would if we worked hard."

"He said within a month," Brin reminded her. "Tomorrow makes only a week."

"Well, since we've been staying later, it seems longer." Kate met Tara's eyes. "I know you told us to wait a week before we asked to stay all day, but we couldn't help ourselves. They even gave us lunch yesterday and today. Anyway, today after work, we were staring at Iron Express over the fence when Mr. Ashman came to see him, and without us saying anything, he saddled him up and led us around. It was a little scary riding such a big stallion. He's kind of skittish around us."

"He said we were naturals!" added Brin, swirling her blond ponytail around her finger.

"Yeah, we didn't ride him alone because he's so feisty, but at least we rode him!" Kate said, doing a little victory dance. "Brin took a picture of me, and I already posted about it on Facebook. I have two hundred comments already!" Kate paused before asking, "Did you ask him to give us a ride?"

Tara smiled, feeling choked up about Crew's actions.

"No, I didn't. Look, I'll share it on the ranch page too. You should tag the page whenever you post about the ranch, so I can share too."

"That would be so cool!" Kate hugged her. "Thanks. And I think I can go back and tag it."

The buzzer rang and the girls insisted on making Tara taste their cookies. "So do you really have a crush on someone at the ranch?" Tara asked Kate.

Kate nodded. "I do. He's seventeen like me and works summers and after school. And guess what? He says he's sure we'll soon be hired for real, when they have openings, but I don't care if we ever get paid because I love it there. That's why we're making these macaroons."

"We heard Mr. Ashman likes them." Brin began dropping more dough on the cookie sheet.

"He does love coconut," Tara confirmed.

Kate scooted her chair closer. "Oooh, tell us how you know that."

"Is he a good kisser?" Brin shot a sly glance at her. "What? Everybody at the ranch is talking about you guys dating. We even heard Isaac saying that he hasn't seen Mr. Ashman smiling so much since his sister left."

The mention of Sophie popped the bubble the girls had been building around her. "What else do they say about his sister?"

"Nothing." Kate rose to put a cookie on a small plate. "Nobody ever says anything. We didn't even know he had a sister until we overheard Isaac talking." She placed the macaroon in front of Tara. "Taste it. Make sure it's good. I hate coconut."

Tara took a bite, wondering if she should leave things

alone with Sophie. What if life got worse for Crew after she told him? But keeping silent now was like a lie, so she would have to tell him. Eventually.

"These are great," she said to the girls. "I'd better take off now. I've got a few things to do tonight. Tell Lily I'll call or come by later in the week."

In the car, she texted Crew: *Thank you for letting the girls ride Iron Express. They are out of their minds crazy about it. You made their day. No, their entire year!*

There was no response, and Tara hadn't expected an immediate one. If he was working in water or mud, he wouldn't have his phone on him.

After her conversation with the girls, the weight of knowing where Sophie was dragged on her guilty conscience. Tara ended up driving back to the Monkey Pants Bar & Grill to see if Sophie was still working and if seeing her might inspire Tara as to how she should break the news to Crew. Maybe she could also probe Sophie about her family to see if she'd changed her mind over the years.

But Sophie wasn't working, so Tara went home, having wasted an extra hour of driving and waiting. She considered texting Marti about seeing Sophie but knew her well enough to think she'd probably march right over to Crew's house and tell him. Tara at least wanted to explain things first.

Explain what? That she was falling in love with him and wanted him to patch things up with his sister so it wouldn't affect their relationship? No way could she admit that. He'd probably run for the hills.

Rylee was in the apartment, eating a salad. "Want some?"

"Sure. I'm starving." She drew her laptop from her bag

and opened it to check on the giveaways she was managing for work as well as those she'd created for Crew.

Rylee grabbed her a diet soda from the fridge. "How's that handsome cowboy of yours?"

"Working. But we have a date tomorrow night." Tara stared at her laptop screen. "Would you look at that? I already have five hundred entries on the horseback riding giveaway. And three hundred on the beef. This is great!"

Rylee laughed. "I hope he knows how much you're working on his account."

"He has no idea." Tara made a face. "It's fun, though."

"Maybe he'll hire you for real part time."

The though had crossed her mind, but now that they were dating, it seemed awkward to bring it up. And if they stopped dating . . . A pit seemed to open up in Tara's stomach.

"Tara, what's wrong?"

Her attention refocused on Rylee. "Nothing, I think I'm just tired, and I still have an ad to mock up for a new account my boss assigned me today."

Rylee grabbed her. "No way. You can do that at work tomorrow. We're going to make popcorn, put on a sappy movie, and paint our toenails or something else equally girly. I know you been busy with your cowboy, but I've missed you."

Tara let herself be dragged away from the counter and her laptop. She did need a break from everything. "You're on, girl!"

On Wednesday, Tara worked through lunch so she could leave at four. She was supposed to drive out to Crew's ranch at six, so this way she'd have plenty of time to get ready. At her apartment, she dressed carefully in a summer dress with strappy sandals, piling her hair loosely onto her head in a way that looked casual, but was definitely dramatic. She felt ridiculously happy just thinking about being with Crew again. How quickly she'd become accustomed to seeing him each day.

When she was ready, she easily had plenty of time to drive to the Monkey Pants Bar & Grill in Tempe if she decided to give talking to Sophie another try. She resisted for all of about two minutes before flying out to her car.

"Is Sophie working today?" she asked a bartender when she arrived.

"Supposed to, but she's not here yet. What can I get you?"

Tara ordered a drink, but twenty minutes later, Sophie still hadn't shown. Time to go if she wanted to make her date with Crew. Maybe she could come back tomorrow or later in the week.

Or she could tell Crew about Sophie tonight. If there was an opening.

She slid off the stool, smiling at the bartender who gave her a little wave as she left. But once outside the bar, tense voices drew her attention. Several yards from the door, a slender young woman wearing black pants and a white blouse was arguing with a big, bearded man—a cowboy from his hat to his boots. From the tenseness of their voices, Tara felt nervous for the woman, who looked like a child compared to his height. His face leaned toward hers, hands slipping around her waist.

The woman spoke and he reacted, pushing her roughly against the building. "You're nothing but a tease."

"Stop. You're hurting me!" The woman pushed back at him, though he was so big, he didn't move an inch. "Go away now, or I'll call the police."

It was that moment Tara realized the woman was Sophie. Fear made Tara's voice tense as she called out loud enough for the couple to hear, "Sophie, is that you?"

The man glanced over at Tara before growling at Sophie. "I got you in. You owe me. This isn't over." He turned and stalked toward Tara, glaring at her as he passed.

Sophie watched him leave, her hands clenched at her side. When she met Tara's gaze, her face was flushed and filled not with the anger Tara expected but with sadness.

Sophie came toward her, stopping several feet away. "How do you know my name—oh, I remember you. The woman with the foal screensaver. You must have a good memory for names." Her hand grazed the nametag on her shirt. "Thanks for coming out here when you did. I'm really grateful. In fact, can I get you a drink? It'll be on the house."

If it had been anyone but Sophie, Tara would decline and be on her way, but what else could she do except follow her inside? This might be the opening she'd been hoping for.

"That guy looks mean," Tara said.

"I can handle him. He's more bluff than anything. He'll cool down."

"Your boyfriend?"

Sophie cracked a smile. "Not a chance. He's got twenty years on me, and like you said, he's mean. He just can't accept the word no. But it was my fault for asking him for a favor. He read too much into it."

Tara wanted to ask what favor, and what he'd meant when he said he'd gotten her in, but Sophie was already going behind the bar. "What will you have?"

Tara shrugged. She didn't really want a drink, but it would give her more time with Sophie. "A soda maybe? I've got a bit of a drive ahead of me, so no alcohol."

Sophie gave her a smile that reminded Tara of Crew. "I can do better than that. Be right back." On her way to get the drink, she stopped and chatted briefly with one of the other bartenders.

Tara pulled out her phone and texted Crew: *Running a little late.* She'd just finished the text when Sophie returned with a drink that looked suspiciously great.

"It's a coconut smoothie," Sophie said, setting the tall glass on a napkin.

"Thanks." Tara took a sip and sighed. "Oh, that's really good."

"So how's your little foal?"

"Good. Growing. But he's not actually my foal," Tara said. "You see, a week ago I went to this ranch to ask if they'd let two foster girls I work with volunteer there, and when the owner was showing me around, I snapped the pictures." She turned back on the phone so Sophie could see the foal. Then she added something she'd learned from Marti. "Apparently, the owner bred this little guy for his sister." She felt daring as the words left her mouth. Would Sophie make the connection?

"How nice." Sophie drew her eyes away from the foal, her smile fading. "Did the owner let the girls come?"

"Actually, yeah. And they're loving it. He's been really kind to them." Tara gulped more of her drink, giving herself a brain freeze. She rubbed her temples regretfully.

Sophie laughed at her expression. "They're best enjoyed slowly."

"I can see that."

"Well, let me know if you need anything."

Tara nodded, still sipping her drink as quickly as she dared. Was Sophie's choice of smoothie related to Crew's love of coconut? Finally, after drinking most of Sophie's concoction, she stood to go. She would only be ten minutes late. Maybe fifteen.

On her way out, she purposefully walked through the bar in a way that would take her closest to where Sophie was wiping down tables. Tara wanted to thank her for the drink, but she couldn't catch her attention.

She was almost to the door when Sophie called out. "Hey!"

Tara turned to see Sophie approaching her. "Thanks again for the rescue."

"I'm glad I was there. And thank you for the drink. You'll watch out for that guy, right?"

"Yeah, I will."

Tara nodded and was about to turn back to the door when Sophie added, "That ranch you're talking about. What was the name? Was it the Silver A?"

The question made Tara realize she'd gone too far. She shouldn't be here. She should have given Crew the information about Sophie right from the beginning, not played amateur detective. What if Sophie ran again before Crew had a chance to see her?

Tara nodded. "Yeah, that's it. Nice people." She wanted to add, "I'm falling in love with your brother so please forgive him and don't run away again."

Sophie was already walking toward the bar. "Have a nice evening," she called over her shoulder.

Tara waited long enough to make sure Sophie was going to help more customers and not run for some back door.

Once in her car, she laid her head against the steering wheel for a full minute before starting the engine. On the way out of the parking lot, she saw a tan truck, and sitting behind the wheel was the man who'd accosted Sophie earlier. Was he waiting until she got off work?

Well, whatever he was planning, Tara knew what she had to do.

11

Crew heard Tara's step on the back deck before she knocked, and he opened the door in a dramatic sweep. "Hello," he said. Her hair was loosely up and her sleeveless patterned dress gently caressed her figure and made her tan skin glow. Her eyes were large enough to be mesmerizing. "You look fabulous." He stepped forward, taking her into his arms.

She gave a low, sexy laugh and lifted her lips to his kiss. She smelled of flowers and tasted even better. "Hmm, coconut," he whispered.

She laughed again. "Yes."

He pulled her tighter, exploring her mouth. Just holding her felt right, as if he couldn't remember how his life used to be a week ago before he met her. "You could have parked out front."

She shrugged. "I guess the parking lot's a habit now. Besides, I like giving your employees something to talk about. According to the girls, everyone is gossiping about us."

"Good," he said. "Let's give them something to talk

about." And he kissed her again for a long while in the open doorway before reluctantly pulling away. "There, that ought to do it. Come on in. Let's get cooking."

"I feel pretty heated already," she murmured.

So did he. He led her inside to where he already had the ingredients to their meal on the counter. Yesterday at dinner, Julie had given him tips on how to prepare the meal, while Isaac and Marti had teased him incessantly. It had been worth enduring their comments to impress Tara.

Tara was still smiling, but her face was clouded, and he knew from experience that meant something was bothering her. Like when she hadn't really wanted to eat the calamari he'd ordered as an appetizer or when Marti had been talking about bungee jumping.

"What's wrong?" he said.

She looked up at him, her teeth biting her lip in a way that made him want to kiss her again, to lose himself in her embrace. "It's not exactly wrong. In fact, I think it's a good thing."

The way her eyes didn't quite meet his made him wary. "What is it? You can tell me anything."

"You really mean that?" She sounded relieved.

"Of course." But a knot formed in his gut, and his chest felt tight with dread. What secrets made her so reluctant?

Tara sat on a stool, laying her bag on the counter. "Well, the other night, Marti told me about what happened with your sister. How she left."

His heart started thudding in his chest. "Okay, I'm sure Marti had her reasons, but how does that affect us?" Even to his ears, he sounded stiff and unyielding.

"I got to thinking that maybe enough time had passed . . . Forget it. I'm just going to say it right out. I found her. I found Sophie."

"You what?" Had he heard her correctly?

Now her eyes dug directly into him. "Marti gave me a picture of Sophie riding Jump Start, and I did an image lookup and found her on Facebook. She works at the Monkey Pants Bar & Grill in Tempe. That's why I was late today. I went there."

"You *talked* to my sister?" Disbelief waved through him, followed closely by anger, the emotions backed by the months of wondering where Sophie was, of how he'd failed her. How could Tara have gone behind his back about this? It felt like a betrayal.

All at once, Tara's face grew shuttered and immobile. She slowly stood, her chin lifting in challenge. "Yeah, I talked to her. In fact, I interrupted a man who was pushing her around, and she made me a coconut shake as a thank you. But I didn't tell her I was trying to find her, if that's what you're asking. She has no idea I know you."

"I don't want to find her!" His hands clenched into fists as he gritted the words.

"Yes, you do!" she retorted. "I see it in your face every time anyone mentions her."

"You had no right to interfere."

"Marti thought it was time. Anyway, Sophie seems like a sweet girl and she's your family. Family!" A hint of passion escaped the mask Tara had pulled over her normally expressive face. "Do you know what I'd give to have *any* family?"

Her words tugged on him, and he felt the urge to

envelop her in his arms again and tell her it was okay, that he didn't mind what she'd done. But he did mind. "The police told me she didn't want to see me."

"That was three years ago!" She raised her hands. "Look, never mind. You're right. I don't have any rights here, and you are free to walk away whenever you want. I'm not holding you back." She turned and swept up her bag. "But just so you know, that guy's waiting for Sophie in the parking lot. On my way out here, I called the bar to let her know he was there, but I'm still scared for her, and if her brother won't do anything about it, I will." She turned in a flutter of her dress and started toward the door.

Everything in Crew wanted to call out to her, to apologize and ask her to stay. But he also remembered the last time Sophie had walked out that same door after saying she hated him, and all the times their mother had gone without a farewell. No amount of tears or begging had worked then.

Tara didn't slam the door behind her as Sophie had done that last day, but let it shut quietly.

Crew's heart hurt but relief wound its way through the hurt almost as quickly like a soothing balm. *Sophie is alive.* She was living her life without him, but she was alive. Thanks to Tara, he wouldn't have to wonder anymore.

Then why was he letting Tara walk away? He raced to the door and flung it opened, but she must have run down the walk because she was already at her car. "Wait!" he called out, but either his voice didn't reach the parking lot or she ignored him. He watched helplessly as she shut the door and drove away.

He sat down at the table on the deck. He'd planned for them to eat out here together and watch the sunset. He'd wanted to tell her he was falling for her, even though it was far too soon. Because he knew she was the one.

Now everything had changed. Would she even talk to him again? A hole that seemed barely patched in his heart had been torn open again.

"You are such an idiot!" Marti's voice carried across the grass.

He dragged his eyes up to look at his cousin, who was striding toward him. What was her problem? "Tara found Sophie."

"I know. I've been working with her. And I just got a weird text from Tara saying you didn't take the news very well."

He gave her an exasperated look. "Why would you do this?"

Marti reached the table and sank into a chair. "Because you bred her a foal. Because she's alone out there. Because she's family."

Her words haunted him, reminding him of what Tara had said. *Do you know what I'd give to have any family?*

"Why are you so stubborn about this?" Mari leaned forward and placed her hand over his.

He stared up at her, wanting to both pull away and to grip her tightly. "What if she doesn't want to see me?"

"Then you tell her you'll stay away until she's ready. Come on. I'll go with you."

Crew didn't move. "I don't mean Sophie." Because as much as it hurt that Sophie still might not want him back in her life, the idea of never seeing Tara again terrified him.

Marti drew her hand away and sat back in her chair. "The sooner you apologize, the better."

His mind kept replaying the conversation with Tara. "Why didn't she tell me she was looking?"

"Maybe she didn't tell you because she was afraid you'd go all werewolf crazy on her," Marti said with a smirk. "Like you apparently did."

He blew out a frustrated breath. "Great. Now she'll never trust me again."

Marti seemed like she wanted to say something more, but she clenched her lips and remained silent.

"What?" he demanded.

"Nothing."

"Tell me."

She leaned forward. "Okay, it's just . . . Tara mentioned feeling Sophie out to see if she was open to us contacting her. I said that was stupid, but Tara was worried about you being hurt. I got the impression from the text she just sent me that she'd been out there several times."

"She should have told me," he growled. "*You* should have told me."

"Uh-uh." Marti shook her head. "You don't get to make the rules. But my point is that Tara went through a lot of effort to try to make things right for you with Sophie. That means she cares about you—a lot. And if you don't do everything you can to make up with her, you're stupider than I thought. Now, come on. Let's go see Sophie before she finishes her shift. We need to talk to her before she decides to disappear again."

Marti was right about that, at least. Crew came to his feet, the decision made. "Okay, let's go. Assuming she'll talk to me at all." But he knew he had the one thing that would get Sophie to listen. Dervin King had called from

High Vista and was eager to seal the deal for Iron Express. He'd sent over the contract today, but Crew hadn't taken it to his attorney yet.

Once in his truck, Crew drove fast, but he didn't go to the Monkey Pants Bar & Grill. Instead, he ended up parked outside Tara's apartment. But would she agree to see him?

Marti peered through the window. "This isn't a bar."

"It's Tara's place."

"Really?" She rolled her eyes.

"What? You said to apologize as soon as possible."

"Well, hurry then!"

He ran up the stairs and banged on her apartment door, but no one answered. Belatedly, he remembered her last words to him, that if he wouldn't do anything to help Sophie, then she would.

Marti was looking at her phone as he climbed back in the truck and started down the road. "She's not there," he said. "I think she's gone to see Sophie."

"Actually, I know that. She just texted me. She says some guy she's worried about is there, but that Sophie has been ignoring him."

Crew felt like a class A jerk. If something happened to either Tara or Sophie, he'd never forgive himself.

By the time he reached the Monkey Pants Bar & Grill, Crew's nervousness had grown to huge proportions. What if Tara wouldn't forgive him? What if his sister called the police when she saw him? What if Sophie was in a relationship with a man who abused her?

The place was crowded and large enough inside that it was difficult to see everyone at once. Music filled his ears, barely heard over a loud group that was shooting pool. Anxiety cranked up inside him. Where was Tara?

"There," Marti said, tugging on his arm.

Crew's eyes fell on Tara, who was sitting at a table with her roommate, Rylee. Tara was talking in that open way of hers, and Rylee was laughing. It should have been with him.

At that moment, Rylee looked and spied them. Her smile vanished as she leaned over to talk to Tara.

"Don't look now," Rylee whispered over their small table, "but isn't that him?"

Tara's gaze followed hers in confusion, because they'd already spotted the big, bearded man they dubbed "Sophie's stalker" at a corner table with four other cowboys.

Her breath caught in her throat as she spied Crew standing near the doorway with Marti, looking in their direction.

"Who's the woman he's with?"

"His cousin."

So Marti had convinced him to come see Sophie, as she hadn't been able to. Tara thought about that for a moment. He'd been angry and hurt—maybe even unreasonably so—but he had come after all.

Because of Marti? Or had he simply changed his mind?

More importantly, what should she do now? Maybe nothing. It wasn't as if he was here for her, though he was still staring right at her.

Tears stung her eyes at the memory of their fight, but

she didn't let them fall. She'd cried all the way here after calling Rylee to meet her, and there were no more tears left.

"He's coming over!" Rylee hissed as Crew started to walk toward them. "What should we do?"

Tara knew from observation that when it came to family, sometimes all reason flew out the window, but the last thing she wanted at that moment was to talk to him.

"Tell him I'm not up to seeing him," she told Rylee. She stood, calculating the steps to the bathroom. Could she hide out there until he left?

Rylee popped up from the table, jumping in front of Crew. "What do you want?" she demanded icily.

"I just want to talk to Tara." Crew's voice carried easily to Tara's ears, despite the noise in the bar.

"She doesn't want to see you."

Tara half expected him to shove past Rylee and come to the table, eyes flaming, and she almost wanted him to because she was angry beneath the hurt and that would give her every reason to lash out.

"Please," he said. He was no longer talking to Rylee, but over her to Tara. "I just want to say I'm sorry."

He wanted to say he was sorry? Suddenly hiding out in the bathroom seemed childish—so not the image she wanted to portray.

Tara nodded and then Crew did push past Rylee, coming to stand in front of her. "Look, I'm sorry," he said. "Really sorry."

"It's okay. I knew I should have told you from the beginning." It wasn't really okay, though. She felt as if there were an ocean between them.

He dropped his hat onto the table and took her hands. He felt so warm, so good, so right, and his closeness made her want to melt into his arms. "Please forgive me." His expression was earnest.

The lump in her throat was too big to speak past. She believed he was sorry, but there was a numbness in her chest right now that she hadn't felt since she'd arrived at Lily's House. She hated how helpless it made her feel. She'd let him get too close. "It's fine," she said. "Forget it."

He smiled. "Okay. So can we sit?" He indicated the table.

Tara was going to tell him she'd have to ask Rylee, but her friend was now at the bar with Marti. Apparently, they'd both decided she and Crew needed some privacy. The phone in her pocket buzzed with a text, but the women were grinning at her and she knew it had to be from one of them, so she ignored it.

Crew and Tara sat at the table. "You came to see Sophie."

He nodded. "You were right. I need to try to talk to her."

Her heart plunged, which was silly because of course he'd come for Sophie. He hadn't even known Tara was there. And Tara wanted him to resolve things with his sister, so she should be happy he'd come.

"But I'm . . . I'm afraid she won't listen," Crew added. "That she won't want to see me. Is she even still here?"

This vulnerable side of him was something she'd never seen before, but she understood what it felt like to be rejected, abandoned, especially by someone who was supposed to love you.

"Left side of the bar, serving that group of women."

He turned and stared behind him for a long time. When

he turned back, there was a glistening in his eyes that hadn't been there before. "It's really her. She looks different."

"Of course she does. It's been three years."

The conversation felt stilted, with none of the ease that normally flowed between them. *They never stay,* she reminded herself. Yet here Crew was, going to face his sister.

Tara stiffened when she saw the bearded man in the corner come to his feet.

"What is it?" Crew asked.

"The man who threatened Sophie just stood up."

Crew scowled and looked over his shoulder. "Where? I'll definitely have a talk with him before we leave."

"You really think that's a good idea?" Crew was as tall as the bearded man but had nowhere near his bulk.

"It's a *great* idea." His voice was a protective growl that touched something in Tara's numb heart. Even if her actions had destroyed their relationship, at least she'd helped reunite him with his sister. If it worked.

"Is he the guy at the bar?" Crew sounded murderous.

She looked again at the bearded man, and saw that in the seconds she'd been talking to Crew, he'd gone to the bar and had replaced the women Sophie had been helping.

"Yeah, that's him. And Sophie looks upset." Before she could stop herself, Tara jumped to her feet and hurried to the bar. Crew called after her, but she didn't wait to hear what.

As she arrived at the bar, Sophie was glaring angrily at the bearded man. "Go away!" she hissed. "I swear I'll call the police!"

"You heard her," Tara said, bumping up against the bar in her hurry. "Get lost!"

The man rounded on her, cursing under his alcohol-laden breath. "No, you get lost! This is between us."

Tara looked at Sophie. "Call the police. He's not going to leave you alone."

More cursing and then from the corner of her eye, she saw the big man's fist coming at her. She started to cringe.

Smack!

Crew's open hand stopped the fist. He stepped between the bearded man and Tara, forcing him back. The bearded man swung, but Crew was faster. His fist slammed into the man's face. Then he grabbed the front of the drunken man's shirt and bent him backwards over the bar. "Stay away from my sister! Stay away from both of them."

He yanked the man upright and propelled him toward the exit. "Now get out of here." With a fiery backwards glare, the man fled.

Crew turned around to face Tara. "Are you okay?"

Tara had to admit that she was shaking. She tried to speak, but Crew's arms went around her, pulling her to his chest. "It's okay." His hand kneaded the back of her neck, and she closed her eyes a moment, feeling pure bliss.

"I take it you two know each other?"

They broke apart to see that Sophie was staring at them from behind the bar.

"Sophie?" Crew said. There was his sister, staring at him, looking so different, yet not different at all.

"Hi, Crew." Sophie looked back and forth between him

and Tara, as if waiting for an explanation. She didn't look angry, though, so maybe that was a good sign.

"Please," he said. "Can we talk? And before you ask, I've found a way to get Jump Start back for you. I know it wasn't right what happened, but I didn't know how to fix it then. I do now."

Sophie's fingers gripped the bar. "And how's that?"

Crew stood taller, taking a deep breath before he spoke. What he was about to say would hurt, but it was the only way. "I'm trading Iron Express for him."

Beside him, Tara gasped. Did she know how much Iron Express meant to him? While he might ride another horse for work every day, Iron Express was his friend.

But Sophie was his sister. Family.

"Are you crazy?" Now Sophie did look mad. She hurried around the bar, resembling a small tornado. She grabbed his hand and pulled him to the end of the bar, next to the door leading into the back.

"No, I'm not crazy. Dervin's been hounding me to get Iron Express, and he seemed pretty happy when he called me back about my offer."

Sophie looked horrified. "You didn't sign anything, did you?"

"Not yet. But I thought you'd be happy to get Jump Start. What's up with you?" Would anything he do make her happy?

"High Vista is on the brink of collapse," she said in a rush. "It's inevitable. You know how hard it is to make a breeding farm successful, and they thought spending hundreds of thousands of dollars in marketing would mask the fact that

Jump Start is really their only high caliber horse. Plus, the breeding fees are being mishandled and aren't making it back to investors, so all of them have pulled out except the owner's father, and even he's cut off any more funds. But if you give them Iron Express, they might be able to recover. Iron Express's breeding fees are triple those of Jump Start's. That's why they made the deal with Dad in the first place. They thought they were getting Iron Express. I don't think Dad knew Grandpa had deeded him to you already."

Crew stared down at her, emotions running through him. Anger at his father, hope that what she was saying might be true. Hope that they'd go back to being friends. "How do you know they're failing? I mean, Dervin's been hot to get Iron Express for years, but that doesn't mean he's in financial trouble."

Sophie thumbed at the exit. "That man you just threw out works for them. I made friends with him so he could get me in to see Jump Start. And he did." Her face turned bleak. "You should see what they've done to him. All penned up. Excessive breeding. I mean really over the top. He looks miserable. But if they fail . . ."

"Jump Start comes home."

Sophie nodded, tears glistening in her eyes. "Even if they don't fail, I would never expect you to give up Iron Express. I know what he means to you."

"But when you left, you said—"

"I was hurt. I wanted everyone to hurt like I did." A tear rolled down her cheek. "It means a lot that you'd give up Iron Express. Really, a lot. But I don't want that."

"I've missed you." Crew held out his arms.

That was all the invitation Sophie needed. She launched

herself at him and he swept her off her feet in a hug. "I'm sorry," she whispered. "I was just so angry, and then . . . I didn't know how to end it."

Crew fought back tears, but they came anyway. In that instant, the weight he'd felt since his family had fallen apart was lifted. "It's over now," he said as he put her down.

Sophie's face was wet with tears. "I hear you have a foal for me. Is it true?"

Tara must have let something slip. Could that have prepared Sophie for this moment? "Yeah. Jump Start's his grandsire and his sire is Iron Express. I know he's not Jump Start, but . . ."

Sophie reached up and shushed him with her hand. "I'll love him." Her eyes went beyond him to the bar. "Who's the girl? Someone special?"

Crew nodded. "Yeah, but I don't know if she'll have me. I've been a bit of a jerk. She's the one who found you. She and Marti." He turned around and as if by cue, Marti was already heading their way. Sophie gave a little squeal and ran into Marti's arms.

Crew watched them for a long moment, as they talked, heads close together. Why had he waited so long to try again?

He turned to thank Tara, but she was no longer at the bar. He scanned the room, only to find that new people had claimed their table and she was nowhere to be seen. Rylee was still at the bar, talking with a man.

Crew fought panic. There was still so much to say. He had to find her.

Tara slipped from the bar, happy it had all worked out for Crew and Marti. She brought out her phone to text Rylee that she was leaving. Meeting here in separate cars did have some advantages. Outside it was dark, though the lights in the parking lot made it feel safe, especially because the bearded man and his tan truck were nowhere to be seen.

She unlocked her car, threw in her keys, and read the text Marti had sent her earlier: *I know he's clueless, like most guys, but just FYI, Crew did go to your house first before coming here. If that matters.*

Tara stared at the text. It did matter. It mattered an awfully lot, though she knew it probably shouldn't.

A shout made her turn toward the building. Crew was jogging across the parking lot, and her heart leapt in her chest before she could tell it to behave. "Why are you leaving?" he asked.

She shrugged. "It's been a long day. I think you need some time alone with your sister."

"I'd really like you to stay." His eyes looked warm and pleading in the darkness. "Or we can go back to the house and finish our dinner."

"Look, Crew, I really like you." *Too much.* "But we come from different worlds." The next words were harder. "I don't think this will work out between us. I don't know that I can ever . . ." *Trust anyone to stick around.* Some of the numbness must have worn off her heart because her words made it break.

"So you're a liar." His eyes flashed.

That stung. "What do you mean?"

"You said you did well with challenges. Well, I know we hit a bump in the road tonight, and I was a jerk, but I'm falling in love with you. I may never have known hunger or what it's like to be shipped off to yet another foster family, but I know what it's like to be abandoned. I know what it's like to cry because your mother didn't want you and your father cared only for himself, even to the point of destroying his family's future. I also know what it's like to stand and fight, and Tara, make no mistake, I'm fighting for you. I learned something tonight—that you can't give up on relationships when they mean everything. They're worth every effort even when it seems all is lost. I need to fight for them like I did my ranch. So you can go ahead and leave right now, but I want you to know that I'll be calling tomorrow and the next day and the next day. Unless you tell me you really don't want to see me again. Because it doesn't matter how long it takes, where you go, or what you do, I'll be here when you're ready to pick up where we left off. I can't promise I'll never be stupid again, but I'm certainly going to try."

She broke then, going to him, letting him envelop her in his strong arms. His lips fell to hers, searching, tentative. Then moving with more confidence as she kissed him back. "I'm falling for you too," she whispered. She couldn't say the word love, not yet. But maybe soon.

"Good." He bent down and picked her up, setting her on the hood of her car as he continued to kiss her. "Because already I don't think I can live without you."

She wanted to tell him he wouldn't have to, but that was too many words. Instead, she just kissed him again.

 EPILOGUE

Three months later

When Tara arrived at the Silver A Ranch for another horseback ride with Crew, he was already waiting at the training barn with Iron Express and Dancer. Tara noted the parking lot was fuller than normal and there were more horses out in the training field.

She was working part-time now for the ranch in marketing, and loving it. The ranch's preorder beef sales were higher than they been in five years, and with High Vista going out of business, they'd also filled their boarding stables to capacity. Crew had been urging her to leave her other job, but she couldn't quite let go of it yet. Because while things were really good between them, they hadn't talked about a future together. And the words "I'm falling in love with you" weren't quite "I love you."

He took her in his arms for a lengthy kiss. "I missed you."

"We just had dinner last night."

He kissed her again. "I still missed you."

"I missed you too."

"Hi, Tara!" Sophie came from the barn leading Jump

Start, whose coat shone almost pure silver in the sunlight. In the four weeks that Jump Start had been back, Sophie had been at the ranch every day.

"Nice boots. Are those new?" Sophie's grin stretched ear to ear.

Tara laughed. "Yep. I finally gave in to the madness."

"I'll buy her a cowboy hat next," Crew threatened.

"You'd better not!" Tara faked a growl.

Sophie dissolved into laughter. "Well, when you finish your ride, come see the foals. I've taught Express Jumper some new tricks."

Crew snorted. "I've told you. He's a horse, not a dog."

Sophie tossed her head. "When he grows up, he's going to be a champion jumper. You'll see."

"I'd love to see him. I'll meet you there." Tara waved as Sophie mounted Jump Start and road away.

Crew stared after his sister. "It's so good to see them together. And guess what? Today, she said she's finally moving back in."

"That's wonderful. Now you won't have to worry so much about her."

"Yeah, and what's more wonderful is that Dervin from High Vista took all his cowboys back to California, including Sophie's stalker."

"That is a relief." The bearded man had come around to the bar once more, but after Crew encouraged Sophie to file a restraining order, he hadn't bothered her. That still hadn't stopped Crew and Tara from worrying.

"Ready to go?" Crew asked.

"Just need to say hi first." Tara ran her hands along Dancer's coat, murmuring hellos. The young mare was also an offspring of Iron Express, but she didn't have Thorough-bred genes from her dam. As far as Tara was concerned, she was perfect.

She swung up on the horse. "Where are we going?"

"Oh, just for a ride." His voice sounded a little too casual, but when she looked at him, he smiled and shrugged.

"Okay, race you!" She leaned forward and signaled Dancer with her feet, and the mare gladly started forward.

They galloped down the grassy road, and Tara felt happy with the wind blowing through her hair and Crew at her side. She couldn't imagine anything better.

They ended up as they almost always did in the upper meadow where Crew had played as a child. He took her hand as they walked across the field. Wild flowers still clung to life even during the hot summer, reminding her of Crew and how he'd held onto the ranch.

She wasn't surprised to see that he'd set out another picnic, but she was surprised when he opened the basket, drew out a cowboy hat, and went down on one knee. She peered inside the upturned hat to see an intricately woven, white gold ring with a large, square diamond. All at once she couldn't breathe.

Crew gazed up at her. "Tara Levine, I love you with all my heart and soul. I want to spend the rest of my life making you happy. Will you marry me?" He drew out the ring and held it above the hat.

She knew the ring was his grandmother's because she'd seen it in pictures. Sophie had talked about how when she married, she wanted a new ring, something all her own, but Tara thought this was perfect. That Crew would entrust it to her meant everything.

"Yes," she said. "Yes."

He slipped the ring on her finger, and then, laughing, pulled her down onto the blanket, where he plopped the hat onto her head. "You have to wear it now," he said. "It's our engagement hat."

She laughed. "Fine, but only on rides."

He covered her lips with his own and tucked her against him on the blanket. Both their hats fell off and neither of them cared. For a very long moment, she lost herself in his touch.

"I love you," he said, pulling back slightly to meet her gaze. "I will never stop loving you."

In those eyes that still reminded her of warm nights and laughter, she saw their ending. And he was there next to her. Never failing, never running away, never backing down from challenges. Always putting his family first, even when they hit bumps in the road. Or ran into the occasional mountain.

She blinked back happy tears. "I love you too."

Up next is Tara's roommate's complete romance. Hope you enjoy Rylee's story!

RYLEE'S
MIX-UP

1

Rylee Williams paused at the corral, studying the pigs. A few chased each other around energetically, huffing and snorting, while others piled in a corner by the food trough, sleeping in a clump. She squatted down next to the corral, and a couple of the curious creatures ambled over to investigate. But when she put her hand through the narrow bars, they snorted indignantly and ran away, one of them letting out a little squeal.

Laughter bubbled up in Rylee's throat. Coming to the Coconino County Fair in Flagstaff had been a good idea. She'd have to thank Keaton Seeger for the invitation to stay at his family's ranch while she was in town for the weekend, as well as for the recommendation to see the animals at the fair, especially the pigs. They were, as he'd promised, the most fascinating animals she'd seen today.

Too bad Keaton had a girlfriend, because thoughtful, good-looking men like him were few and far between these days. The last three guys who'd asked her out, she'd turned down flat. She'd known their type—handsome and handsy, she called them. Not her style.

Her roommate, Tara Levine, who was recently engaged to Crew Ashman, owner of the Silver A Ranch in Phoenix, had offered to set Rylee up with some of the hands who worked for her fiancé, but Rylee wasn't interested. Besides, Keaton was the only guy working for Crew who had ever dared talk to her. And he was taken.

"Cute little critters, aren't they?"

Rylee lifted her gaze to see a man jumping down from a small tractor hitched to a large wagon that hadn't been there moments earlier. She straightened, and still had to look up, which was nice because she was on the tall side for a woman, and while she had on her new tennis shoes this morning, she loved wearing heels.

"They're adorable actually," she said. "Like awkward little babies. Only they aren't really babies anymore, are they?"

His blue eyes filled with laughter. "Nope. They're weanlings. But they still act a lot like babies." His hair under the tan cowboy hat was brown and a few days' beard growth made his face ruggedly handsome. He looked familiar, as if she'd seen him somewhere before, but she knew she hadn't. She'd remember a man like him.

He was staring at her every bit as much as she stared at him, and she couldn't help flushing, feeling suddenly self-conscious.

The stranger nodded, giving himself a little shake. "I'm Beck," he said, offering his hand.

"Rylee." She let his hand envelop hers. For some reason she was finding it hard to breathe. Probably just the Arizona heat that was already in full swing this placid Friday morning.

"Nice to meet you." He dipped his head, lifting his hat

a few inches like a character from an old movie. "Hope you're enjoying the fair." He turned to the gate, his muscles rippling as he opened it. Was he going inside?

"Yes. It's interesting," she said.

Sure enough, he ventured inside the corral, his hands held out as if to catch any pigs that might try to flee. He didn't need to worry. They all scurried to the other side of the pen.

"Hey, you mind giving me a hand?" His eyes wandered back to her.

"Sure. I guess. Doing what?" She really hoped he wasn't going to give her a cheesy line or make a pass. They'd only just met.

"I need someone to stand here and make sure none of them escape while I back the wagon in."

"They're going somewhere?"

His laughter was deep and friendly, sending odd little flutters through her stomach. "They have a performance soon."

She arched a doubtful brow. "Performing pigs?"

His grin deepened. "Not exactly."

What could it hurt? The pigs didn't look like they weighed more than twenty pounds, so it wasn't as if she would be in danger of getting trampled. Rylee took Beck's place in front of the gate, waving her hand at a pig who approached. It darted away with an affronted snort that made her laugh.

Beck was already up on the tractor, backing the wagon inside the pen opening, which seemed to be a close fit. She doubted any of the pigs could escape through the sides. But under the wagon was apparently a juicy temptation because a few of the piglets were approaching her position cautiously, their eyes focused on the opening.

"Shoo," she said, waving her arms as Beck stepped from the tractor into the wagon and then jumped into the pen next to her. He let down the tailgate, and as he did, the pigs rushed past Rylee, snorting and squealing in their hurry to scurry up the tailgate and into the wagon, where they began gulping something from a trough.

"That was unexpected," Rylee muttered, thinking that in retrospect, they'd looked a bit large and dangerous as they stampeded past.

"I hadn't given them breakfast yet. They know the drill."

"All but him," Rylee thumbed at one runt, still lying in the corner of the pen.

"Yeah, that one always needs a little priming." He pulled something from the pocket of his shirt. "Want to do the honors?"

"Sure."

He tossed her something that looked suspiciously like a dog biscuit. "Just hold it out on your hand."

Walking around a clump of straw, Rylee approached the pig. Squatting down, she called, "Here, Wilbur."

"Wilbur?" Beck asked.

"From Charlotte's Web."

"Yes, of course. Except she happens to be a girl."

"Wilma then."

"Always loved the Flintstones."

Little Wilma gave a loud snort and jumped to her feet, her snout twitching. Then in a move almost too fast to follow, she snatched the biscuit from Rylee's hand, inhaled it, and sniffed around as if looking for more.

"Sorry," Rylee murmured.

With an aggrieved snort, Wilma dodged past her and darted up the tailgate into the wagon with the rest of the pigs. Beck deftly lifted the tailgate and pushed it shut. "Thanks," he said.

"You feed your pigs dog biscuits?"

"A vegetarian dog biscuit, I'll have you know." He stepped toward her. "But, no, they normally eat grain. That was just a treat."

He was looking at her with eyes she could drown in. Maybe she was already drowning because she couldn't for the life of her remember what they were talking about. Oh, right, the pigs.

"So where are they going?" she asked, wetting her lips.

"Greased pig contest."

"What?" Her thoughts abruptly refocused. Keaton had said something about making sure she didn't miss a certain pig contest that his family sponsored. Maybe this was related. "But isn't that a little barbaric?" she asked.

He gave her a look that clearly said, *Oh, you're one of those nut jobs.* "And eating them isn't? You do eat pork, right?"

"Yeah, but I don't chase it first."

His smile showed he was more amused than offended at her comment. "Don't worry. I assure you, it's quite humane. When I was a kid, we had to drag the pig to the judge, or stuff it in a burlap bag. All we do now is attach a dollar bill to a collar around its neck. The kids just have to rip it off."

That did sound more humane. "Still, they're being chased and greased."

He laughed, a genuine sound that made her want to join in. "Those pigs have grown up chasing kids or being chased by kids. It's a game for them. And it isn't the pigs that are greased."

Rylee didn't quite understand what that meant, but she didn't want to appear to be a total idiot by probing further.

"How about you give it a try?" he asked.

"Me?" Was he serious? And why did it seem as if he were suddenly too close and too far away at the same time? "I don't think so."

"Chicken?" His eyes didn't leave her face.

"Maybe a little." A lot, actually. Of him at least. Her insides were doing a funny jig, something she hadn't felt in a long time but recognized. She was attracted to him in a big way. If she were smart, she'd walk away.

So, of course, she didn't.

"Want to come along and help with the collars?" He glanced over his shoulder at the wagon, filled with snorting pigs. "It's for charity," he added, as if she needed encouragement to spend more time with this handsome cowboy who made her heart pound and her thoughts suddenly desert her.

"Okay. But only because it's for charity."

He laughed again. "Ah, and I thought it was because you couldn't resist me."

That was so close to the truth that she decided a change of subject was in order. "So, you come here every year?"

"Oh yeah. This is big for our ranch. We sponsor a 4-H club, and they show their animals. We also sponsor booths and contests, which help us make important connections in the community."

"Contests like the greased pig thing?" She wondered if he worked for Keaton's family or another ranch nearby.

Either could be possible with the amount of people here. She'd have to ask.

"That's right." He climbed into the wagon before she could phrase her question. "I'll just move this so you can get out."

After wading through the pigs to get to the tractor, he moved it a few feet and then jumped back down and offered his hand to help her into the tractor seat. She took it, startling a little at the way her heart seemed to settle at his touch. As if she was right where she belonged. He released her far too quickly, and for a few scattered seconds, she stared at her hand.

"What about you?" he asked as he slid next to her on the seat. "You been here before?"

"This is my first time." She thought about saying more, how she'd come to Flagstaff to attend the wedding of a sister she'd never known, a sister who hadn't been abandoned to strangers like she had. But no, that was far too personal.

The hot sun beat down on them as they drove through the fairgrounds. People waved friendly greetings at Beck over the growl of the tractor. Young children stared, and a few ran along beside them. Delicious aromas wafted on the light breeze and made Rylee remember she was hungry.

"You're pretty popular," Rylee commented.

"They're just jealous and hoping I'll introduce you."

This close, she could see the way his eyes crinkled at the corners when he smiled. "Yeah, right."

He chuckled. "I only tell the truth."

All too soon they arrived at a larger corral where half a dozen kids and a beautiful young woman waited for them. The woman carried a basket full of paper strips that looked a lot like the carnival wristbands Rylee had seen on many of the youths at the fair today.

"Finally," said a girl of about eight, who had long brown pigtails reaching halfway down her chest. "We still got to put on all their collars, and people are already here." She gestured to the clumps of fair-goers who were gravitating toward the corral.

"Plenty of time." Beck jumped to the ground from the tractor and turned to help Rylee down. "Besides, I brought help."

"Oooh," the little girl mocked, while a couple of boys barely out of their teens whistled.

"Don't mind her," the beautiful woman said, pushing past the children with an outstretched hand. "Nice to meet you. I'm Nora, Beckham's sister and the 4-H leader of these ragamuffins. The loud mouth belongs to me." There was a family resemblance, especially in the dark hair and braids that Nora also sported, but she didn't look old enough to be the little girl's mother.

"Nice to meet you," Rylee said as they shook hands.

"Who wants the first one?" Beck asked. He and two of the kids, including Nora's child, had already climbed into the wagon and now held wriggling pigs in their arms.

The remaining children on the ground dived for the paper collars and began snugly fastening them to the pigs held by those in the wagon. Then the pigs were set free in the corral, where they happily began wandering around.

"Here's one for you," Beck said, holding out a pig to Rylee that looked like Wilma.

Rylee grabbed a collar from the basket and tore off the backing.

"Make it really snug."

Rylee stopped to examine the dollar bill stapled to the collar. "Wait, this isn't even real."

"Nope. Had too many rip in half. We exchange them for real ones after the contest. Whoever gets the most wins fifty bucks."

"I thought this was for charity." Rylee took Wilma and set her gently in the corral. The pig didn't feel slimy and wasn't nearly as stinky as she'd expected but was a lot heavier. These 4-H kids must be stronger than they looked.

"People pay ten bucks to enter and we pay them from that. We run it several times, a dozen or so people at a time, and only give the fifty bucks to the overall winner. We always raise at least a couple hundred dollars for Nora's program."

"Sounds a bit easy. I mean, to rip off the money."

He laughed. "That's where you're wrong. Most of the pigs manage to keep their dollar bill. But I really think you should give it a try. Remember, it's for charity."

She put another collar on the pig he was holding, then staggered under its weight as she let it down into the corral. "Been eating a little too much, have we?" she murmured. When she looked back at Beck, he was watching her. "I thought this thing was for little kids."

"That's tomorrow. Today it's sixteen on up." His smile was a challenge.

How hard could it be? She reached into her pocket and took out the phone she carried in a thin leather wallet with a credit card slot and a pocket for bills. She pulled out a ten-dollar note and held it up to him. "Okay, I'm in."

"That's Sadie's domain." He gestured to his niece, who

immediately dropped the pig she was holding into a boy's arms, snatched the bill, and climbed out of the wagon.

She pulled a ticket from her pocket. "Here you go."

Nora frowned. "Are you sure about this?" She cast a rather dark look at her brother. "We don't want to chase her away."

"She's good with pigs." Beck swung down from the wagon and a boy took his place catching the few remaining collarless animals. "You might need this." He handed her another dog biscuit.

Rylee rolled her eyes. "Isn't that cheating?"

"All's fair in love and war and greased pig contests." He flashed her another grin, which made her forget what she was about to do. Anyway, the worst that could happen was she'd run around and never get close to an animal.

It's for charity, she reminded herself as she stuck the biscuit in her pocket.

Sadie was already taking tickets from people. She stopped after letting a dozen people in the corral, then motioned to Rylee. "I saved you a spot in this one." She gave a knowing smirk that made Rylee feel a bit nervous.

Nora stepped closer, pushing past her brother. "You'd better give me your phone, if you've got one, just in case." Nora held out her hand and only with a slight hesitation did Rylee pull it out of her back pocket and give it to her. The only thing of real value there was her credit card, and she figured it was safe enough with Nora.

"And you might need this." Nora began removing the elastic from one of her braids.

"But your hair . . ." Rylee trailed off as Nora pulled her other braid around the back of her neck and fastened the elastic on that one around both of the braid ends before pushing them over her shoulder to hang down her back. "Oh, thanks."

Rylee gathered her long blond hair up in a high pony-tail. It was better to keep it clean since she was going to see Marlee and her mother tonight at the rehearsal dinner. *Birth mother,* she reminded herself. It hurt less thinking of her that way. Lily Perez from Lily's House was the woman Rylee considered her real mother, the woman who had taken her in when she was sixteen, ending the flood of foster homes she'd been shuffled off to over the years. Before that, Rylee had stayed only periodically with her birth mother, usually when her mother's guilt sent her to rehab, but it was never for more than a month or two at a time.

Not Marlee, though. Her older sister had stayed with their mother from the beginning, and Rylee couldn't help the resulting load of resentment for both her sister and mother. Why had she even come to attend the wedding? She'd asked herself the question a thousand times.

Because of her roommate. Tara had given her some spiel about meeting her family halfway. Tara saw the invitation as a path to mending the gulf between them, and Rylee had caved. But now she was having second thoughts. No, third or fourth thoughts. She had Lily and Tara and the others from Lily's House. They were all the family she needed.

A warm hand landed on her shoulder. "Having second thoughts?" Beck asked, his voice warm and more than a little teasing. The challenge in his eyes was clear.

If only he knew. "Not on your life, mister."

His answering grin was all she needed to fuel her. Maybe

he was different. Maybe soon it wouldn't only be Tara who was getting meaningful kisses from a cowboy. The kind that hinted of a future. She took a deep breath and joined the other contestants already in the corral. They were mostly teens, but there was a mother with her daughter and a man with his son, so she wasn't the only adult.

"Good luck," Nora said as she approached with a bottle of oil, which she proceeded to pour over the outstretched hands of the first contestant.

So that's what Beck meant by not oiling the pigs, Rylee thought. She held out her hands like the others and let Nora drip oil over them.

Afterward, Nora helped her daughter shut the gate, while Beck hopped back up on the wagon. Someone handed him a bullhorn. "Okay, folks, listen up," he boomed, his amplified voice quieting the crowd. "We welcome you out to the Coconino County Fair and our greased pig contest sponsored by B&K Ranch. Here's how it goes. You have five minutes to grab as many bills as you can off these pigs. Then we'll reset and start the next group. Looks like we'll be running two groups today. Whoever has grabbed the most bills after both contests wins today's grand prize of fifty bucks. There is no second or third place, so there is only one chance!" The crowd cheered.

"Oh, and pigs?" he added, lowering his voice. "Make sure you go easy on these people. No fair making them look too bad."

The crowd thought that was hilarious, but Rylee started to feel a little uneasy. What was she doing? Surely there were easier ways to meet guys.

"Okay," Beck shouted. "Ready, set, and go!"

The contestants took off running. Rylee went one step and then stared down at her new baby blue tennis shoes doubtfully. There were two spots of oil on them already and dust rose up in a little puff around her shoe. Dust came off, right?

"Get a move on!" Sadie yelled at her. "You're gonna lose."

Rylee started running. But every time she approached a pig, it darted away easily, its snort sounding like laughter. She tried to grab onto one, but her greased hands slipped off. This was harder than it looked.

Then the crowd went wild as one teen managed to snag a bill. He punched the air with his fist in jubilation. Seconds later the same boy grabbed another bill. The contestants were becoming creative now in their desperation to win. They tried sneaking up on pigs, walking backward, and even squatting down and calling to them. The mother-daughter team worked together to trap one pig between them, ripping the bill from the collar as it darted past.

Many of the pigs had retreated to a corner and Rylee headed over in that direction. Why wasn't anyone else going for this group? Someone yelled at her to stop, but the animals were just sitting there waiting for her. With so many clumped together, she was bound to get at least a couple of the fake dollars as she waded into them.

She knew the minute her foot hit the straw near the pigs that all wasn't well in this corner of the corral. As she took a few skating steps, she spied a boy with mud all over his pants and suspected he'd been the one to warn her.

Too late. She fell, gliding over the ground like a baseball player sliding into home base. She sailed into the knot of pigs, who moved aside and stared at her mockingly. She could swear they were laughing at her. Like the crowd that was hooting loud enough to make a person go deaf.

The pigs didn't seem to mind the noise, but they were slowly edging away from her. Rylee wasn't about to let that happen. Still on her backside, she whipped out the biscuit Beck had given her. The nearest pig gave a greedy snort and stepped toward her.

"Wilma?" Rylee asked.

As if the porker was going to answer.

Rylee ripped the bill from the pig's collar, then held the biscuit in the direction of another pig. It snorted and the next thing she knew, several animals were playing pig tackle. She closed her fist over the biscuit and fought a scream.

Just her luck, she'd finally met a man who might be worth dating and she was going to die of bacon smothering before he ever asked her out.

2

One minute the intriguing stranger was sailing across the corral and the next she was down, sliding on the mud. Beside Beck, Sadie slapped her leg, chortling in a manner that her mother had cautioned her against on numerous occasions.

"It worked. It worked!" She jumped up and down as if to emphasize the words.

"You did that?" Beck asked.

Sadie beamed proudly. "Hey, on the flyers we told all the entrants to bring a change of clothes, didn't we?"

Beck didn't respond. Things in the pen were getting worse. Rylee had managed to grab a bill, but the pigs had gone crazy, pushing up against her. One of the boys, half covered in mud himself, dove at a pig and ripped off a bill, raising it triumphantly.

No one paid attention because everyone was riveted on the girl in the middle of the pigs. *Great,* Beck thought. *I'm going to get her trampled to death.*

He leapt from the wagon into the corral, hitting the

ground at a run. By then the rest of the contestants were converging upon the group of pigs. Three more people went down in the mud. Beck could hear Sadie laughing above the crowd. She was going to get it when he finally caught up to her. For now, he had to save the woman.

The next minute Rylee jumped to her feet, laughing as she ripped bills from the pigs. Beck slowed as two more people skidded across the mud, both coming up with a bill and cheers from the crowd.

Rylee lifted a hand full of bills as someone sounded the ending horn. "I got a few," she called to Beck.

"So I see," he called back.

She slopped through the mud toward him. Her clothes were an utter mess, and there was mud on the ends of her hair and splashed across her cheeks. She looked even more beautiful and compelling than when he'd first seen her. He had the wild urge to run up to her and kiss her, mud and all.

He took a deep breath and moved closer. "And here I was thinking you'd just find Wilma and give her the biscuit."

"Not on your life. She was laughing at me!" Rylee held out her other hand, revealing the biscuit.

He laughed. "Well, I see you taught them who was boss."

She shoved the bills at him. "Oh, they're nothing compared to the kids I grew up with."

"Can't wait to hear about them."

Her smiled wavered. "Nothing to tell. Just bullies. I like pigs better."

There was a story behind that, he could tell by the hint of sadness in her face, but now wasn't the time. He offered his arm. "Let's go see how you did."

She'd ended up with four bills, one more than the next in line. Beck shook his head in amazement. "That might just win it for you," he said, "if the last group isn't faster."

"Well, I did cheat a little with the biscuit. So it hardly seems fair to the others." Her gaze dropped to her clothes, a line appearing on her brow. "Hey, is there anywhere I can wash up?"

Beck signaled Sadie. "My niece will show you where."

"But I got another set of contestants," Sadie whined.

"Go," Beck ordered. "We'll take care of it. And while you're gone we'll also try to clean up your mess. And for the record, I don't even want to be around once your mother gets a hold of you."

"But it was funny! Everyone thought so," the child protested, her eyes going to her mother, who was exchanging real bills for the fake ones the contestants had gathered.

"Oh yeah?" Beck thumbed at Rylee. "Ask her if it was funny."

Sadie didn't look at Rylee but at the ground as she mumbled a subdued, "Follow me."

As they left, Beck heard Rylee say, "It was kind of funny."

Beck wanted to kiss her again when Sadie laughed and grabbed Rylee's hand.

Nora finished paying out the bills and came up to Beck. "This was my daughter's prank, wasn't it?"

"Of course it was Sadie. That's why I made her go help the girl clean up."

"I bet she'll never go out with you now." Nora made a face.

Beck felt a sudden worry. "Hey, she was laughing."

"Yeah, only to keep from crying. Man, why did you

make her go in there?" Nora punched his arm. "Lame, lame, lame. You need to stop your teasing."

"I don't know. She seems different from other women."

Nora stared at him. "Different how? You mean like when I met Jim?"

Exactly like that, but Beck felt saying it aloud would jinx everything. Nora had been engaged to marry another man when she'd met Jim, and after knowing him only two hours, she'd broken her engagement and accepted a date with him. Six months later they were married.

"Well," Nora said, her eyes wide. "I see."

He moved away. "I'll get more fencing inside to keep the pigs from the mud. There's biscuits on the tractor seat if you need them." They'd have to entice the pigs over so those that needed to could receive new collars." They'd all need a bath when this was finished.

He had barely started the next contest when Sadie returned with a rather soggy-looking but still attractive Rylee. The growing tension inside Beck faded. She'd come back. That was something, wasn't it? Though maybe she only wanted her fifty-dollar bill.

When she smiled at him, his thoughts scattered. "Want to get a bite to eat when we're finished here?" he asked, jumping down from the wagon. No use leaving these things to chance.

She looked over her mud-stained clothes. "Like this?"

"I'm not worried about it if you're not."

She laughed. "Sure. I'd say you at least owe me lunch after making me mud wrestle a bunch of pigs. I think my shoes are ruined."

She was probably right. "Sorry."

"I'd believe you a little more if you weren't smiling." She elbowed him in much the way his sister might have.

He was doing an awful lot of smiling, but he couldn't seem to help it when she was around. She was crazy attractive yet down-to-earth friendly, unlike a lot of women who looked like she did.

"So, Rylee, where are you from?" he asked as they stood watching the other contestants try to grab the dollar bills from the pigs.

"Phoenix. I'm just here for the weekend."

Phoenix wasn't too far away at least. "Meeting?"

"Sort of. A family thing." Her nose twitched as if smelling something sour.

"Not good, huh?" He was more curious than he wanted to let on.

"I guess I'll see. Anyway, I'm glad I came here today."

"I'm glad you did too." Their gazes locked for a long moment until the cheers from the crowd directed their attention to the corral. Beck wished he could take her away already.

Nora sounded the ending timer and the collected bills were counted. One teenager with acne had grabbed five.

Rylee looked relieved. "Easy come, easy go," she quipped. "But too bad for your sister. I was going to donate it to the charity if I won."

Getting the pigs back into the wagon was harder than it had been the first time, but with the help of the 4-H kids and some of their parents, they shooed all the pigs inside, even Wilma.

"I'll drive them back to their pen," Nora said, "and warn the people who are next in line for this corral about the mud." She glanced at Sadie. "And you're grounded, young lady."

"Yeah, yeah, yeah." Sadie heaved a long, aggrieved sigh and climbed up on the tractor.

Rylee was doing her best to hide a smile as mother and daughter drove away. "Sadie said she and another kid let the water run for two hours and then spread the area with fresh straw. Apparently there was a slight indentation on that side that was perfect for collecting water."

"My niece is very inventive."

"She's cute too."

"Yeah. She is." They both laughed.

Beck let his feet lead him in the direction of the food booths, and before he realized it, they'd ended up at Hot C-Dog, which had the hottest chili dogs in pretty much the entire world. "Uh, no," he said. "Maybe not here."

"Why not? I love chili."

"These are really hot."

She dipped her head forward and then back, her body following the motion in a slight wave. "Bring it on."

So they ordered chili dogs and double-sized drinks and sat together on a bench. They ate as their eyes teared and guzzled the soft drink to wash away the most unbearable part of the heat.

"These are not for the weak," she said. "I'd love to introduce them to my foster sisters."

"Foster sisters?"

"Yeah, especially Tara, my roommate. We spent time at the same foster home, and she's still my best friend."

A foster home. That would explain the vibe he'd received

when she talked about why she was in Flagstaff. "It was a good place, I hope."

"The best. At least that one." She smiled and pulled out the phone Nora had returned to her. "Here's a picture of us then." She scrolled through to one that showed two teenage girls, the slender one with blond hair obviously being Rylee, who was beautiful even then. "She's engaged now."

"I think my younger brother's heading that way," Beck told her. "We're close too. Always have been, except for a few months in college when he stole my girlfriend."

"Stole your girl, huh?"

He laughed. "Yep. It was for my own good. At least that's what he told me at the time. He dumped her a week later."

"He probably did you a favor."

"A big favor, actually."

"So, do you like the girl he's dating now?"

"Haven't met her yet, but soon." Today, in fact, if Beck had understood his mother correctly. His brother's girlfriend was coming to town this weekend to attend a wedding, and he'd asked to let her stay at the ranch until he joined her on Sunday when he had a special announcement for them—probably that he intended to marry her. It was odd to Beck that his brother wasn't going with his almost-fiancée to the wedding, and letting her meet the family for the first time alone seemed insensitive. But he didn't know anything about her and the dynamic between them, so it wasn't his place to say.

"My brother's in Phoenix now," he added. "He's working at a cattle ranch there to learn the ropes to help our own business grow. Our family has been raising various kinds of animals for decades, but we're pretty new to cattle, and we want to avoid the worst mistakes."

"That's smart." She ran her tongue along her lip to catch a bit of chili. It was all he could do to remind himself that they barely knew each other, and kissing her out of the blue wasn't going to win him points in his favor.

The buzzing of his phone pulled him from his thoughts. "With all we've got going on at the fair, I'd better check who this is." He glanced at the phone, squinting at it in the bright light. "Speak of the devil. It's my brother. Do you mind?"

"Of course not. Go ahead and talk to him. I'll just throw our stuff away." She gathered their wrappers into the fast food sack and started walking to the garbage can down the path.

"Hello?" Beck answered his phone.

"So, how'd the pigs go?" Keaton asked.

"Just like it always does but with a bit of added mud, thanks to Sadie."

"Why am I not surprised?"

"Because it's Sadie. But guess what? I might have met someone."

"No way! Really? Finally. What's she like?"

"Well, I could be imagining it, but everything about her is perfect so far. She liked the chili dogs, and she entered the pig contest. She fell in the mud and laughed about it." He chuckled at the memory.

"I knew right away Lee was the one for me. Like Nora did with Jim."

"Lee?"

"That's all you're getting out of me until Sunday. You'll

love her, I promise. I was only with her two hours before I knew she was something special."

"Well, I need more than two hours."

His brother laughed. "Okay, you can have until I get there on Sunday. You kiss her yet?"

"That's rushing things, isn't it?" Beck glanced up and saw Rylee coming back. She moved with an easy grace, looking all the more adorable for her stained clothing.

His brother was saying something about their ranch, but Beck was no longer listening. He only caught the words "Be kind to her, okay? Give her directions, and if she needs a plus one for anything connected with the wedding, go with her? When I get there, I'll tell you more."

"Yeah, don't worry about it. I'll take care of her for you. Gotta go. Bye." He hung up and pocketed the phone.

"You're smiling," Rylee said. "Must not be serious."

"I think he just called to make sure I'd be nice to his girl."

She laughed. "You mean so you don't throw her in the mud or anything?"

"Something like that." He cleared his throat. "Uh, why don't I show you around?"

"Okay, but I only have maybe an hour. Two tops. I need to get cleaned up before I meet my sister." The way she said *meet* seemed significant, as if meeting her sister wasn't something she did every day and possibly something she dreaded.

"Sister?" he asked, trying to sound casual.

They walked a few steps down the path before she responded. "Yeah, she's my older sister. Three years. My only sibling. But we never really lived together."

"That's where the foster homes you were telling me about came in?"

Her eyes met his, seemingly troubled, and he wished he could take back the words. "I went to a foster home when I was a few months old," she said. "My sister stayed with my parents. Apparently, it was easier to hand over a baby than a three-year-old you were already attached to."

What could he say to that? "So your parents were together?"

"Yeah. For a time, anyway. I don't think they were ever married, though. I went to live with them for two months when I was five, and that's the first real memory I have of them. There might have been other visits before that, but if so, I don't remember."

"Why only two months?" Maybe he shouldn't ask, but he really wanted to know everything about her.

"I was in kindergarten, which meant half the day, and when the social worker learned I was home alone during the afternoons, she sent me back into foster care. The idea was that I'd return to my family when I was in first grade, but my dad went to prison and died there, and my mom had to work more hours, so that sort of nixed the idea."

"I'm sorry."

"Don't be. I didn't know him, and his death wasn't traumatic for me. I spent a few months on and off with my mom after that, but it was always better when I wasn't there. I really didn't have it all that bad." She smiled, and he didn't know her well enough to judge if she was only masking the pain or telling him the truth. "I know you hear horror stories, but the two foster homes I was in before turning five were really pretty good. If my mother hadn't insisted she was working toward custody, either of those families would have adopted me. The homes after I was five were not as great but okay. I had social workers helping me. It was only a few of my teen years that were difficult."

"That sounds about like every teen I ever knew. But I'm sure it was worse for a foster kid."

She shrugged. "Mostly it was because I was so outspoken. You learn to remain silent or be loud in the foster system, and I was loud. Plus, my foster brothers suddenly wanted to be more than brothers, if you get what I mean, but I'd seen girls abused and my social worker had made me take a class on abuse. I ratted 'em all out—and punched a few too. That's how I ended up at Lily's House. They take in only girls."

Beck had no trouble imagining her receiving unwanted attention from pubescent boys, and though the offenses were far in the past, his fists itched to teach a few of them a lesson.

Something in his expression made her laugh. "It toughened me up, which has served me well in my career as a mortgage broker. By the way, if you ever need a loan, I'm the one to come to. I always get the best rates."

He chuckled as he sensed she wanted him to. "I'll remember that."

They walked around, looking at the animals, crafts, and the baking competitions. They even went into the handling area and held some of the petting animals. Rylee was almost convinced to buy a baby rabbit but held strong at the last moment.

"Where would I put it?" she said.

"Not at your apartment, that's for sure. But you can come see the ones we have at my ranch any time."

"About your ranch," she began. "I've been meaning to ask . . ." Her words trailed off as she spied something behind him. "Oooh, look! Cotton candy. It's been years since I've had any." She reached for her pocket, presumably for payment, but he put a hand on her arm to stop her.

"Let me," he said. "My treat."

She smiled, her eyes so compelling that he couldn't look away. "Okay," she said softly.

He felt like he'd been given the world instead of permission to buy her candy. Maybe his brother and sister were right. Maybe she was it. He expected terror to enter his heart at the idea, and when it didn't, he laughed.

"What?" she said, arching her brow in a way he'd begun to recognize and anticipate.

"Nothing. But I do love cotton candy. I have some every year here, though usually my niece is the one to insist on it."

He bought two bags of cotton candy, not knowing if she'd be okay sharing like he and Sadie normally did. He managed to finish all of his as they perused a few more booths, but she finally handed him the rest of hers.

"Guess I have more eyes than stomach. It's sweeter than I remember."

He put it back in the bag it had come in. "You can take it with you for later."

"Speaking of that, I hate to say this, but I really need to get going." She pointed down at her mud-streaked jeans. They were dry now and most of the mud had fallen off her tennis shoes, but she did still look like she needed a good washing. "The rehearsal dinner tonight is best dress. And before that I have a fitting."

"A fitting?"

"Didn't I say? I'm apparently going to be a bridesmaid at my sister's wedding."

Wedding. That was an interesting coincidence, since Keaton's maybe-fiancée was coming to town for a wedding as well. Lee or whatever her name was. Maybe she was friends with Rylee's sister. A warning prickled the back of his neck, but he pushed it away.

"I'd probably better get back to my duties too," he said. "Nora's good at keeping track of things, but she'll need help with her 4-H gang, and I have a few contacts I need to catch up with."

"Well, thank you for an interesting time."

He felt a sudden rush of panic. If she left now, he might never see her again. "Can I call you?"

This time her smile seemed a bit shy, which was so far from the confidence she'd shown thus far that it further intrigued him. "I'd like that."

He put her number in his phone. "I'll send you mine too," he said. "If you get done early at your sister's thing, give me a call tonight."

"You won't be here until late?"

"Not very. Plus, there are others who can help."

"Okay then."

They stood awkwardly, people pushing past them. Time seemed to freeze. His heart might even be skipping beats, if his sudden disorientation was any sign.

She pushed up on tiptoes and gave him a hug, which he returned with more enthusiasm than her gesture merited. She felt good in his arms. Too bad he had to let her go.

"Here, don't forget this." He handed her the cotton candy.

Her grin turned his stomach upside down. "Thank you."

Turning, she sauntered away, and he watched her until she disappeared into the crowd. Only then did he remember that at some point he'd have to go back to the ranch to welcome Keaton's girlfriend. But their mother was home, and as distracted as she'd been since her fall from the horse, she was well enough to receive a visitor. The housekeeper was coming in every day now instead of once a week to help until she was healed, and together they'd probably spoil his brother's girlfriend so much that he wouldn't be missed if Rylee called tonight and wanted to do something with him.

Right now he had to hurry, or he'd lose out on seeing Sadie showing her cow. Whistling to himself, he hurried along the path.

3

Rylee was flying—at least that's how it felt. Never mind that her new shoes were ruined, grit was between her toes, and she was a little buzzed by all the sugar from the soft drink and the cotton candy.

And from the look in Beck's eyes.

He liked her. He hadn't gone all weird when she'd talked about her family or the foster homes. Yes, she'd downplayed the bad years, but those times had contributed to making her who she was every bit as much as the good homes had. She was proud of surviving, of making the best of her life despite the difficulties.

She was feeling rather silly for having spent hours talking to Beck without learning if he knew Keaton's family, and whether he owned his own ranch or if he managed one. He was obviously in some position of authority, but the subject hadn't come up naturally, and she hadn't wanted to seem as if she were pushing for financial information. The only thing she knew is that whatever his job, he was involved with sponsoring contests at the county fair.

Well, all that would have to wait. Now she needed

to find the ranch where she'd be staying, and she should have Keaton's address here somewhere in her text. There it was, the B&K Ranch. It sounded familiar somehow. Beck might have said that name when he started the greased pig contest, though she'd been a little too preoccupied to hear much of his announcement. Had he mentioned other sponsors?

It didn't really matter. He had her phone number and would call.

Unless he didn't. She frowned. No. She couldn't have imagined his interest, could she? Only one way to find out—she'd call Tara and see what she thought.

Tara answered on the first ring. "Hey girlfriend, what's up?"

"I'm not sure. Remember how Keaton said something about his family sponsoring booths and events at the fair?"

"Yeah. Quilts and a pig contest. And there might have been something about 4-H kids and cakes."

"You remember more than I do. Anyway, I went looking for the pigs and I met a guy."

"Wait, what? A guy with pigs?"

"It's better than it sounds, though I did fall in the mud when I was trying to rip off the bills."

"Slow down! I have no idea what you're saying."

So Rylee recounted every delicious moment, from the time she'd first met Beck to their hug goodbye. "What I didn't get around to asking was if he was connected to the B&K Ranch or another sponsor."

"I can ask Keaton."

"No! Don't you dare! Promise me you won't say anything until I find out if he's even going to call me."

"I thought you were supposed to call him if you finished early at the rehearsal dinner."

"Whatever! I don't want Keaton butting in and getting me a charity date."

Tara laughed. "I understand that. I just hope you actually get a chance to call him while you're there."

"Me too. I really like him. I don't know if he's in a position to be serious or anything, but I'm not in a hurry."

"If you don't call him, I bet he'll call you," Tara said. "But tell me the most important thing. Did you get a picture of yourself covered in mud? Because I could really use it to make a post for the Silver A's Facebook page. And Twitter, of course."

Rylee laughed. Tara had worked in marketing before she'd met her fiancé, and even before they'd fallen in love, he'd been smart enough to elicit her help reworking his ranch's public image. She'd already helped increase his beef sales substantially. "Trust you to be thinking about that. I had his niece take a picture with my phone. I'll text it to you."

"No, email it. That will give me a better resolution."

"Okay, but I'd better go now. I'm still a mess, and I have to shower and get to the dress fitting before Marlee's dinner."

"Wish I could be there with you."

"I'd say going with your fiancé to see his estranged mother for the first time is probably a bit higher on your list. Besides, Marlee wasn't exactly generous with her invitations for my friends." Rylee had paid for one extra meal from her own pocket, thinking she might take a guy she'd been dating or Tara, but by the time she knew the guy wasn't going to work out, Tara had made plans with Crew and his mother.

"Well, it's taken Crew two months to agree to even speak to his mother, so you're right, but I know this is big for you. Doing this with your birth family, I mean. Do you know who you're taking yet?"

"I ended up asking Jason from work. He's the only one I trust since we're friends. He's not busy, but he's trying to convince his girlfriend I'm not out to seduce him. He'll let me know in the morning."

Tara laughed. "Sorry, I know it's not funny. But maybe you can ask the pig guy."

"Don't call him that! His name's Beck. Short for Beckham, I think his sister said."

"Okay, okay, but meeting him the way you did is kind of romantic."

"We'll see. I definitely like him, but I need more than a few hours to fall for a guy. Goodbye now. I'm hanging up."

Rylee followed the directions to the B&K Ranch. It was on the outskirts of town and had a long, paved driveway leading to a white farmhouse with a wide covered porch and two steep gables. In the front was a circular cobbled driveway and a small patch of grass surrounded by a flowerbed. Green fields bordered the house, one of which held half a dozen grazing horses.

She climbed from her car, enjoying the fresh air and the breeze that softened the still-burning sun. It had to be after three already, which meant she barely had time to get ready before her fitting at four. Then she'd have an hour or two to kill until the rehearsal dinner at the groom's family's house.

Rylee had missed the bridal shower last month, though

she'd sent a present, and she knew she should have been happy she hadn't been expected to plan the shower, but at the time all she'd felt was sad that she didn't even know Marlee's favorite color. Part of that was her fault, but Marlee hadn't made any effort either. Until now—and Rylee wasn't sure how much of that was their mother's doing. She'd recently remarried, and that might factor into why she had dragged Marlee with her to track Rylee down in Phoenix two months ago to deliver the wedding invitation and to exact her promise to attend as a bridesmaid.

"Easy," Rylee told herself. She breathed in the peace surrounding her. The place looked so calm, so idealic that she snapped a few pictures for Tara.

Fighting the urge to explore, she removed her suitcase from the trunk of her car, hefted it to the porch, and climbed up the stairs. Garden furniture adorned the space, looking comfortable and inviting. Fleetingly, Rylee wished she could sit down and take a nap, despite the heat. Or maybe because of it.

She rang the bell, which sounded imperiously throughout the house. She hoped no one was napping. A voluptuous Latina woman with graying hair and bright eyes answered. "May I help you?" she asked in heavily accented English.

"I'm Rylee, Keaton's friend. This is the B&K, right? I'll be staying here for the weekend?"

"Yes, yes. Come in, come in." The woman opened the door and grabbed Rylee's suitcase from her hand before she could protest. "I am happy to meet you. Keaton's mother . . ." She rambled off something Rylee didn't catch.

"I'm sorry?" she asked.

The woman laughed and put her palms together near

her cheek. "Sleeping. You see her tonight." Her eyes traveled down Rylee's clothes with interest.

"Sorry I'm such a mess. I fell in some mud at the fair."

"No problem. Take off your shoes here. I will clean."

"Oh, you don't have to do that. I'm not sure they can be saved. But I do have someplace to be in an hour. I have a dress fitting."

"*Vestido de novia?*" The woman waved her hands down her ample body.

"Um," Rylee hedged.

"Dress for wedding?"

"Yes, that's right."

"Oh, good!" she squealed with entirely too much excitement, and Rylee couldn't help thinking something was missing in the translation. She should have paid more attention to her Spanish classes. Some of the girls at Lily's House had even tutored her, but right now everything she'd learned seemed beyond recall. Fortunately, the housekeeper was smarter than she was about languages.

"Come. I show you to the room." The housekeeper beckoned, and Rylee followed her to a beautiful upstairs room that had obviously belonged to Keaton. A banner with his name and the framed picture of him on a bucking bronco were dead giveaways. A queen-sized bed covered with a beautiful blue-toned quilt stood near a large window.

"When Keaton comes, he will sleep in his brother's room," the woman said. "Not together. Not here."

"Of course not." Did the woman think she had designs on Keaton?

The housekeeper looked relieved. "Good." She pointed down the hall. "Bathroom is there."

"Thank you so much. I'll just shower and get out of your way."

"You eat dinner tonight?"

Rylee only understood the woman because of the accompanying eating motions. "No. I'll be with my sister for dinner. Please don't worry about feeding me. It's really just nice to have a place to sleep."

"Ah, *niña*, it is a pleasure." She patted Rylee's cheek, lapsing into Spanish that was somehow comforting.

"Thank you."

Left alone, Rylee ran to the bathroom for her shower. If she washed her hair, she wouldn't have time to fix it before the fitting, and that meant going to the rehearsal dinner looking like someone who had just stepped from the shower. She'd been aware of that when she'd made her choice to stay with Beck, but now she regretted it a little. She wanted to make a good impression on Marlee and her soon-to-be in-laws.

She ran her fingers through her hair, testing the cleanliness. She'd gotten the mud out, and it didn't feel horribly heavy with dust. If she set it instead of washing it, and used a lot of hairspray, she might be able to make a good appearance. She opted for the curlers and added a heavy dose of perfume, just in case there was any lingering *eau de cochon* from her encounter with the pigs.

Hopefully, it would be enough.

4

The fitting took place at a bridal shop, and Rylee went alone. With the wedding happening tomorrow, all the other women in the wedding party had been fitted weeks ago. Any significant changes couldn't be accommodated this soon before the wedding, and Rylee hadn't wanted a fitting at all, trusting the sizing, but Marlee had insisted and it was her day, so Rylee had made this appointment. She didn't expect to wear the expensive dress again anyway.

When she saw the narrow cut of the floor-length gown, she repented of that thought. The teal color was eye-catching, and the cut would show off her slender figure.

Or would have if the dress had been the right size.

Rylee blinked back tears as she stared at herself in the mirror. The dress was at least two sizes too large and she looked rather like she was playing dress-up in her mother's clothes. "I don't understand," she said. "I always take a size six."

"Oh, this is a ten." The attendant looked at the order form. "They come in even sizes."

"I know I told my sister a six." Rylee took out her phone

to check her texts. "See?" She showed the woman, who nodded sympathetically.

"I'm sorry, but that's not what was ordered, and while it's usually easier to take in a dress than let it out, there's no way our seamstress can adjust it by tomorrow afternoon."

"What if I paid extra?"

"She's not even in until Monday. However, I do have a few decorative pins that might help make it usable."

Rylee sighed. "Okay. Show me how to do it and add them to my bill." Hopefully her sister wouldn't be upset about the additions.

"You might be able to find someone else to take it in. Do you know anyone who sews?"

If she'd been back in Phoenix, Lily would probably figure something out, but Rylee didn't know anyone here. "Maybe," she said. With the rehearsal dinner tonight and the bridesmaid brunch tomorrow, finding someone didn't seem possible.

She took the dress, glad she hadn't trusted her sister with picking out the matching heels. At least those would fit.

She drove around town, stopping at a few dry cleaners to see if they could alter the dress in time. But after four visits, she gave up and went to the rehearsal dinner. Signs pointed her around the back of an elegant two-story house that had beautiful flower gardens lining the walkway. In the grassy back yard, a large canopy had been set up over round tables, and fans directed cooling air toward the gathering occupants.

Rylee was impressed and glanced down to make sure her pink skirt and white blouse weren't wrinkled. At least she wasn't underdressed.

"Rylee!" Her mother swooped down on her, though it took a moment for Rylee to recognize who she was. Kimberlee had lost a lot of weight since they'd last seen each other in Phoenix. There was also no trace of gray in her blond hair, and her makeup was more subdued. Her face was still a bit haggard, but she looked better than Rylee had ever seen her.

"Hi, Kimberlee." Rylee returned the awkward hug. Instead of love, she felt a familiar rush of anger at seeing this woman who hadn't been able to get it together enough to raise her but had been selfish enough to prevent her from being adopted by any of her foster families.

"Hey, everyone, I want you to meet my younger daughter," Kimberlee announced, slipping an arm around Rylee. "She's a mortgage broker. She graduated from finance in college."

Murmurs went around the tables, and some of the older ladies nodded in approval. "Her name is Rylee," Kimberlee added with a giggle. "Get it? Kimberlee, Marlee, and Rylee?"

Marlee made a little sound and moved through the tables quickly, giving Kimberlee a warning stare. She wore an elegant dress with ultra-tall heels that made her almost as tall as Rylee. Her blond hair hung in carefully arranged ringlets, and she was even wearing pearls. She didn't look like the girl who had stolen Rylee's lunch money when she was eight and who gave her pot when she was ten.

Suddenly, Rylee understood that her sister was marrying up in the world. Rylee herself had always imagine getting married in a church and having a dinner afterward in Lily's back yard. For rehearsal dinners, if they even had one, the Lily's House girls usually held their own barbecue and wore pants. They were accustomed to making their own bridesmaid dresses, arranging their own flowers, and cutting corners. This was not going to be that kind of wedding. No wonder the bridesmaid dress had cost nearly two hundred.

"Thank you for coming," Marlee hugged Rylee. "You got the dress? How did it fit?"

"Fine."

Marlee grinned. "It's good that I ordered two sizes up then, isn't it?"

"Uh, well." Rylee forced a smile.

Marlee gave an excited little bounce, and her ringlets jiggled with the movement. "I didn't imagine that you were really a six, being so tall and all. I can barely fit into an eight."

"You look wonderful, dear," their mother said. "And it's so good to have us all together. Rylee, you have to meet my husband, Leo. Oh, there he is now."

A short, stocky man strode toward them, a smile on his face. "Leo Knox," he said. "Nice to meet you. I see beauty certainly runs in this family."

"Thank you. Nice to meet you too." Rylee's proffered hand was enveloped by his.

Leo put his other arm around Kimberlee. He had short brown hair speckled with gray, warm green eyes, and a slightly pointed chin. He was somewhat shorter than both of them in their heels, but it didn't seem to bother him. He gazed at Kimberlee adoringly. "Come on. Let's go sit down. They're about to start the toasts."

Kimberlee nodded. "Rylee, you're at the bridesmaid's table. We'll show you."

Rylee let herself be dragged under the canopy to a

padded chair in front of a dinner salad and a roll. The four other bridesmaids were there, along with their dates, and a younger girl who looked about ten. Rylee felt a moment of awkwardness at seeing the other girls with dates because her sister had specifically told her the rehearsal dinner was only for the wedding party and immediate family. No dates. Well, it was probably a good thing since she wasn't even sure if she'd have a date for the actual wedding tomorrow.

"I'm Elena Sweeny, Marlee's maid of honor," said a girl with shiny ebony hair. "And also her best friend. This is my date, Adrian."

Rylee smiled. "Nice to meet you."

Elena introduced the others in rapid succession, but Rylee didn't fix any of the names except the little girl, Molly, who was Elena's younger sister.

The little girl leaned closer, her eyes shining. "Isn't this tent wonderful? My mom ordered it."

"Oh, I see. So you and Elena must be the groom's sisters." Their last name had seemed familiar, and Rylee had probably seen it on her invitation. "Is this your mother's house?"

Molly laughed. "Yep. I live here too."

"I'm glad to meet you finally," Elena said. "I've been bugging Marlee about you since I learned she had a sister. She kept putting me off, and we were all starting to believe there was something strange going on, you know? But here you are."

Rylee nodded, relieved that she was prevented from answering when the father of the groom gave a toast and invited everyone to begin eating. Rylee ate her salad, which was soon replaced by a plateful of something she hoped was chicken.

While they were still eating, Kimberlee was invited to say a few words about Marlee. Then it was the groom's mother's turn to talk about her son, Calvin. A few others offered toasts or stories of how they met the groom or bride, wishing them a long life full of happiness together.

One of the bridesmaids at Rylee's table whispered, "Boring!" She signaled the waiter for another glass of wine as the others laughed.

Aside from their initial greeting, Rylee didn't talk to her mother or sister. She had the distinct feeling that she didn't belong here, that she was an afterthought, and she wished she hadn't agreed to come. They weren't family, not really. They were strangers.

But her mother and sister seemed different from even a few months ago. When had they changed? Each time she'd been taken to live with them for a few weeks or months as a child, she'd always reminded herself that it wouldn't last, and it hadn't. They'd never changed, and in the end, Rylee had been sent away again.

She wasn't going to count on their change meaning anything this time either.

Pushing the thoughts away, she busied herself trying to eat, but nearly choked when she realized her chicken salad was actually some kind of crab. Maybe it was her uncertain upbringing and youthful reliance on macaroni and cheese, but she'd never developed a taste for seafood. Somehow, she managed to get a bit of it down, though all the while she was wishing it was one of the hot chili dogs she'd eaten that afternoon with Beck.

"Ah, this is delicious!" Kimberlee's voice sailed over the tables to Rylee a little too loudly. Next to her, Marlee put her hand on her arm with a sharp smile. Kimberlee just laughed and sipped more wine.

The servers brought cheesecake for dessert, which almost made up for the crab. Rylee hadn't tasted cheesecake before moving to Lily's House and she still couldn't get enough of it. Two of the other girls at the table refused to eat the dessert, and the others only ate a few bites. Rylee savored hers and accepted another piece offered by the waiter.

The dinner dragged on, but Rylee was in a calorie-ridden sugar haze that made it all okay. Finally, the talking stopped and the caterers began whisking away the remains of the food. Rylee arose and weaved through the chatting crowd, looking for her mother. Instead, she saw Mrs. Sweeny, mother of the groom, who stood on the patio near the back door of the house. She had a little twitch to her nose and her eyes were narrowed, her mouth unsmiling.

Rylee followed her gaze and saw that she was staring at Marlee. Maybe she wasn't as happy at the nuptials as her speech had indicated. But Rylee repented almost immediately of the thought. Just because she harbored resentment toward her family didn't mean others felt the same.

But maybe she could leave now. Or soon. It was only eight, which meant plenty of time to do something else. She pulled out her phone and texted Beck. *You still want to meet up?* It wasn't exactly the phone call he'd invited, but it was all she could do at the moment.

She finally caught up to her mother near a decorative bush chatting with her new husband. "Do they need any help cleaning up?" Rylee asked.

"Oh, no, the Sweenys' caterer will take care of that." Kimberlee sounded pleased with the idea. "Did you meet Calvin?"

"No, he and Marlee seemed kind of busy."

Kimberlee frowned. "I can take you over."

Now that her mother had pointed it out, it did seem rather odd that her sister hadn't brought her fiancé over to introduce him, but Rylee hadn't made the effort to seek him out either. "It's okay. I'll chat with him tomorrow. The wedding's at four, right?"

"Yes. But you need to be at the club by two for pictures. You still have the address?"

"Yeah, on the text you sent. If I'm not needed, I'll take off. It's been a long day already, and I know there's a lot going on tomorrow. Looks like things are winding down here anyway." Some of the guests had already begun leaving.

Kimberlee's eyes ran over her face, as if searching for some kind of slight. Rylee stood awkwardly under her scrutiny, hoping her desire to flee wasn't apparent.

"Okay, sweetie," Kimberlee said finally. "Thank you for coming. It's so good having my girls together again."

Sweetie? That was new, and not a sentiment Rylee appreciated, even if it was only for Leo's benefit. If she'd ever been Kimberlee's sweetie, it had only been when she was newly born, when Kimberlee had given Rylee the matching "lee" in her name. Before Kimberlee had decided she couldn't handle another baby. Which, admittedly, had been more than true.

As for being together again, Rylee fought the urge to say, "Yeah, I almost didn't recognize you without the messy ponytail and the beer in your hand."

Instead, she smiled and said, "I'll see you tomorrow at the bridesmaid brunch?"

"Oh, that's just for you young girls." Kimberly put an arm around Rylee, the alcohol on her breath noticeable. "But we'll be seated together tomorrow at the wedding dinner. The tables are larger and rectangular, so they'll fit both of our immediate families and dates. You do have a date, right? I know Marlee said you didn't have one for today, but Leo paid a plus-one for you tomorrow."

Leo had paid? Then why had Rylee sent Marlee seventy bucks for an extra plate? "Yeah, I do." Or maybe she did.

"We're just lucky the Sweeny family is picking up the tab on their own guests for tomorrow and the open bar," Leo said with a hearty laugh.

Kimberlee shushed him. "Not so loud."

He shrugged. "Well, it's true. And it's only fair since they're the ones planning most of it."

"They just want to be involved. It's a good thing."

Obviously, there was some undercurrent here that Rylee didn't understand, but she had a good impression of Leo. He seemed caring and down to earth.

Kimberlee looked as if she wanted to say more, but she didn't. She simply smiled and watched Rylee walk away. Without a scene. Relief flooded Rylee. There had always been scenes with her family, ones that had left the child she'd been breathless with hope or anger or dejection, depending on the circumstances. Tonight she walked away mostly unscathed. Maybe she could do this. If she could just get away without blowing up with Marlee about the dress—or showing jealousy.

Because she *was* jealous. Not of the wedding or the

money Marlee was apparently marrying into, but because of the new family Marlee was getting. They were normal, if a little too refined. They were people who wouldn't have abandoned their child with empty promises.

Okay, so maybe Rylee wasn't quite unscathed, but she didn't feel unhappy. How could she on a day when she'd eaten cotton candy, chili dogs, and two pieces of cheesecake?

Rylee's phone buzzed before she arrived at the car, and she hurried to unlock her door and slip inside.

Love to, Beck had replied. *Where should we meet and when?*

I can get away now. You choose the place. I'm not familiar with anything around here.

What part of the city are you in now?

Rylee texted the address and a few minutes later the response came. *How about Collins Irish Pub and Grill? That's nearly in the middle between us.*

Rylee did a quick search on her phone. *Sounds great,* she told him. *It will take me fifteen minutes.*

It will take me at least that. I should be there by 8:30.

See you then.

She punched start on her phone's map and pulled from the curb. This night wasn't a complete disaster. There had been no scenes at dinner, she had a nice place to sleep tonight that didn't cost her an arm or a leg, and she was on her way to meet a handsome cowboy.

Rylee had always considered the description of butter-flies in the stomach a gross exaggeration, but she changed her mind on the way to the pub. Her stomach was doing all sorts of odd things, though that could be overload of cheesecake.

She arrived first and went inside to see how crowded it was, but before she'd made it far, Beck called her name and came toward her from the entrance, touching his hand to his hat in greeting. He looked more than good, and she was glad she'd taken the chance to text him.

"Busy place," she said over the noise.

"I'll get us a table. It's usually open seating, but on busy nights it pays to check." He winked at her and crossed to the hostess. After a short chat, she led them to a booth.

"I'll get someone to serve you right away," she said with a flirtatious smile at Beck.

Rylee laughed. "Looks like she's a fan."

He shrugged. "I got the prettiest date here. Even without the mud, which I kind of liked."

After the tense evening, the comment was exactly what she needed. "Thanks. You look good too." He'd changed to dark jeans and a button-up shirt, which did everything to emphasize his broad chest.

"What will you have?" he asked. "I'm a little hungry, and their burgers are really good."

"Well I did have dinner. Sort of."

He cocked his head. "Sort of?"

"It was crab. I guess I never developed a taste for it. I did eat two whole pieces of cheesecake."

"Then you definitely need a hamburger to get rid of the sugar rush."

As if on cue, a waitress appeared. "What can I get for you tonight?"

"I'll take your Texas barbeque burger, and one for my date, if she'll give it a try." He winked at Rylee. "Unless you want something else."

"I'll try it," she said.

While they waited for their food, she talked about the rehearsal dinner and how she pushed the crab around on her plate and chomped down cheesecake while the others pushed theirs aside.

"I can just see you gathering up all the leftovers to take home," he said with a generous laugh.

"I was tempted. The family my sister is marrying into is really nice. I'm happy for her. I just grew up a little differently, that's all."

"Tell me about it."

So she talked about going to Lily's House when she was sixteen and how she'd met her best friend Tara there. "Lily is one of those people I aspire to be like," she said. "She takes in everyone. Gives them the benefit of the doubt. Basically, she loves them into submission."

"Sounds a lot like my mother," he said.

"Tell me about her."

But their food came then, and for a while they were busy eating. "Mmm," Rylee said between bites. "I don't think I've ever had a better burger."

"I know, right? Try the fries."

Rylee did. Beck got started talking about his niece, Sadie, and how the cow she'd raised from a baby had taken second place at the fair. "She's madder than a rattler in a rainstorm at that," he said. "Her worst enemy from school took first."

"Poor thing," Rylee said.

"I told her it was the universe doling out her punishment for the mud prank." He rolled his eyes. "As you can imagine, that went over really well. Oh, wait a minute," he added, pulling out his phone. "I'm getting a call. I wouldn't take it, but it's my mother, and she's not feeling that great."

"Go ahead." Rylee was glad he didn't ignore his mother.

"Hey, what's up?" he said into the phone. "Oh, yeah. Again? Yeah, I know. Tell her I'll be there soon." He hung up, looking remorseful. "I'm really sorry, but I need to go. My mother fell off a horse and broke her leg a few weeks ago, and we don't like to leave her alone."

"She's not doing well?"

"She's doing fine, but she won't stay down. If we leave her alone, the next thing we know, she's out trying to feed the horses or gathering eggs from her prize chickens. One time I found her standing on the counter on one leg cleaning the cupboard. She has a lady who comes in to help out when I'm not home, but there's been an emergency and she has to leave early tonight."

"Well, of course you need to go." Rylee hoped her disappointment wasn't showing and that this wasn't some weird excuse to end their date.

"Thanks for understanding." He signaled the waitress. "But you know . . ." He looked at her, his eyes looking midnight blue in the stark light of the pub. "I'd rather be with you."

The seconds stretched out between them, signaling something good, something right. Did he feel it? Yes, by the expression on his face, he felt it as much as she did.

"Hey, I know," he said. "You could come home with me. If you don't have to get back to where you're staying, that is."

"I could come for a while, but I shouldn't be out too late because I'm staying with the family of a friend." As it was, Rylee might have to text Keaton to see how late his family normally stayed up. She didn't want to inconvenience anyone.

"Maybe I'll be able to change your mind about leaving early." His grin made her feel like flying. "My mother plays a mean scrabble."

She returned his grin. "Maybe."

She couldn't decide if it was weird or endearing that he was taking her to meet his mom, but she was glad the evening wasn't quite over.

They stood to leave and his hand closed around hers as they navigated the pub. Outside, he didn't let go. "Where are you parked?" he asked.

He walked her to the car, the moonlight bathing them with a romantic shimmer. Everything felt magical. "Should I follow you there?" She pushed the unlock button on her key fob.

"Sure. I'm down that way." He opened her door, hesitating a moment as he stared down at her. The look in his eyes . . . he was going to kiss her—and she wanted him to.

He bent toward her slowly. Her heart pounded. His lips found her cheek, his touch warm and tantalizing. "See you soon."

She fought disappointment. Not exactly the kiss she'd expected, but the words sounded like a promise.

Rylee called Tara on her speakerphone as she drove behind Beck's truck. "Guess where I am right now."

"At the rehearsal dinner holed up in the bathroom with an extra slice of cheesecake."

Tara knew her so well. "Haha. No, I'm going back to Beck's place or his mom's. I'm not quite sure which."

"No way. Tell me everything."

By the time she did and Tara had gushed appropriately, Rylee was beginning to recognize the road they were on. She hadn't asked Beck about his connection with the B&K Ranch, but it was obvious that he or his mother lived nearby. An uneasy feeling started in the pit of her stomach, though she couldn't pinpoint why.

When he eventually turned down the paved drive to the B&K Ranch, she said, "Um, Tara, do you remember what Keaton's brother's name was, or if he was married? He did say his mother lived at the ranch, right?"

"Yeah, she's a widow. Keaton and his brother live there

with her—or did before Keaton came to train with Crew. Why?"

"Because I just followed Beck to the ranch."

"Oh, wow." Tara was silent a moment. "Well, that makes sense. Their family sponsors stuff at the fair every year, and Keaton told you to look for the pigs, and that's where you met Beck. And of course he lives with his mom. Or she lives with him. What's he going to do, make her move out just because he's running the place now? Their father died some years back, if I remember correctly."

"I wish I'd made the connection before. I mean the way he talks, I figured out he was running a ranch, but I didn't think it was Keaton's. It seems kind of like I was hiding the fact that I'm staying at his house."

"No, it doesn't. It's funny, and if he's anything like Keaton, he'll laugh and say it's fate. Have fun! I'm hanging up now."

Was it fate? That made Rylee smile. She stopped her car behind Beck's parked truck, and turned off her phone, tucking it into her pocket. Beck was already nearing the porch. Probably anxious to check on his mother. He was a good son.

She popped the trunk and climbed from the car. Might as well bring in the dress and explain everything. Hopefully, Tara was right and they'd all get a good laugh.

What was taking Rylee so long? Beck had parked in front of the house instead of pulling into his newly-built garage. He should have waited for her instead of hurrying to the house, but he was seriously worried about finding his mother washing the floor or trying to carry a basket of clothes down the stairs. The last thing she needed was another broken bone. Seriously, sometimes he thought she was fifty-four going on fourteen. She was determined to do whatever she wanted. Hopefully, Delfina, the house-keeper, hadn't left yet.

His body tingled with anticipation of being with Rylee again. He'd been tempted to kiss her in the pub parking lot, but that wasn't the way he wanted his first taste of her. She was special, different from anyone he'd ever met, and he wanted it to be memorable. He was falling—fast. But it didn't scare him. It felt right.

Rylee was coming toward the house now, after having retrieved a dress bag from the trunk of her car. That was a little strange, but maybe she wanted to show him the dress she'd bought for her sister's wedding or was worried about the dress getting wrinkled. She was so beautiful that for a moment, he stood there, drinking her in. Was this how his siblings felt before they fell in love? Was it how his father had felt when first meeting his mother?

His hand was on the doorknob when her foot hit the stairs. He'd asked Delfina to keep it locked, but sometimes she forgot. They didn't have much trouble out here.

"Beck," Rylee said, her smile bright. "There's, uh, something I should tell you. It's funny, really. Just realized it myself when you pulled up here."

"Oh, yeah?"

Before she could continue, the doorknob twisted under his hand and the door flew open.

"There you are," Delfina said. "*Finalmente!* Good because I have to go. Josefa thinks she's in labor . . . again. She is not, but you know how she is. Your mother . . ." She shook her head. "Impossible! She wants to go for a walk. A walk in the dark with crutches!" Her eyes went past him to Rylee. "I'm glad you made it back safely, *cariña*. How went shopping for *el vestido?*"

Surprise flooded Beck. Delfina knew Rylee? But how was that possible? Rylee's face looked more amused than concerned, and for some reason that calmed him.

"It went okay," Rylee said to Delfina unconvincingly.

Delfina crunched her eyebrows together, peering through the clear plastic covering Rylee's dress. "Interesting color for a *novia.*" Shrugging, she swept up a black purse by the door and shouldered past them, humming as she went down the porch stairs and off into the night.

"So how does she know you?" Beck asked as they watched her go.

"Beckham," his mother called. "Bring her inside, dear."

He turned to see her balancing on her crutches at the end of the entryway.

"I've been waiting all day to meet Keaton's friend," his mother added, "but apparently I was sawing logs when she arrived this afternoon."

Keaton's friend? Beck heard the words, but they didn't compute. He felt stupid and slow. Rylee wasn't Keaton's friend, she was his friend. He'd met her at the fair. Unless, she was the "Lee" Keaton had referred to.

He turned back to Rylee, who smiled at him as she came inside the entryway. "That was what I was about to tell you. And it's even why I was at the pig corral this morning. Keaton said something about his family and all the contests you guys sponsor, but I didn't realize you were his brother until I followed you here just now."

She said it casually, as if it didn't matter. As if they hadn't held hands when he walked her to her car at the pub. How could she be Keaton's girl and look at him the way she had then? And was still looking at him. How could he feel this way about a woman who was claimed by his brother?

Everything was suddenly wrong.

His mother motioned toward them and Beck had no choice but to walk toward her. "I'm Gracie Seeger," she said, dipping her head. "Keaton and Beck's mom."

"Nice to meet you. I'm Rylee Williams. Thank you for letting me stay here this weekend."

"The pleasure is all ours."

Beck helped his mother to the couch in their family room. He remained standing himself, feeling awkward and unsure if he should confront Rylee. Had he read things between them completely wrong?

No. She'd held his hand. She'd flirted with him. He recognized flirting when he saw it. He wasn't that inept about women.

"Is that the dress?" his mother asked as she pulled her broken leg up on a footrest. "Delfina told me you'd gone shopping for the dress, but I wish I could have gone with you." She stared up at Rylee with excited eyes. "It's an interesting color, isn't it?"

Rylee frowned at the dress. "Is there something wrong with it? I kind of like it."

"It's beautiful," his mother agreed. "It's just unusual for a bride."

Rylee laughed. "Oh, it's not a bridal dress." She untied the bottom of the plastic and pulled it up to expose the entire gown. "It's a bridesmaid dress for my sister's wedding tomorrow." She looked between them as if expecting them to say something. When they didn't, she continued, "Keaton did tell you I was coming for a wedding, right?"

Beck's mother was nodding. "Yes. And it's a beautiful dress for a bridesmaid." She grinned. "You had me worried there for a moment. Only . . ." she trailed off.

"Only what?" Rylee's eyes widened expectantly.

She was so beautiful that Beck had problems focusing on anything else. *She's Keaton's girl,* he reminded himself. *Back off.*

She hadn't seemed to want him to back off earlier.

"That dress looks a little big," his mother said. "Unless you like it that way."

Again Rylee's laughter filled the room. "Two sizes too big actually. My sister thought the size I ordered was too small since I'm so tall, and there isn't enough time for them to tailor it."

"More likely she didn't want you to steal the show," his mother said, rolling her eyes.

"That's kind of you to say." Rylee pushed the plastic back down over the dress. "They sold me some silver broach pin kind of things to tighten it a little. Doesn't look too bad. It's only for one day."

"I might be able to help." His mother heaved herself to her feet. She wasn't a large woman, but with the heavy boot on her leg, everything was an effort for her. He scrambled for her crutches, standing to put them under her arms. "I'm not a seamstress by a long shot," she continued, "but I know my way around a sewing machine. It'll certainly look better than pins. Come with me to my craft room."

"Oh, no. You don't have to do that." Rylee looked uncomfortable. "You should rest."

"That's what I've been doing for weeks. Come along, dear. It'll give us a chance to get to know each other. I've been excited to meet you ever since Keaton told Delfina you were coming."

Delfina had talked to Keaton? He hadn't realized that. Probably his mother had been asleep when Keaton called. She'd hit her head pretty hard in the fall and got headaches if she didn't rest enough.

"But, Mom," Beck began, "maybe it'd be better not to push yourself. Like Rylee said, it's only for one day."

Rylee shot him a grateful look, and he wondered if she was worried his mother would ruin the dress.

"I'm fine," his mother told him. "You stay here. We'll come back after I see what's needed. I'm sure you'll want to check with the boys about the cattle anyway, seeing as you've been gone most of the day." Without waiting for a reply, she began swinging her way across the room on her crutches.

Rylee hesitated, giving Beck an uncertain smile, and he felt a rush of both anger and protectiveness. But his mother's, "Come along, dear," propelled her from the room.

Beck stared after them, not sure whether he should run after her and demand an explanation or sink to the couch in shock. She would have let him kiss her. She would have let his lips explore hers. She would have put her arms around him as he pulled her close. He was sure of all that.

But she was Keaton's girl, and she'd come here before Keaton's visit on Sunday only because of her sister's wedding. There was nothing more to it.

Beck sank to the couch, his knees abruptly unwilling to hold him. What should he do now? He'd have to tell his brother. He had to know.

Know what? A voice inside his head mocked. That Beck had almost kissed Keaton's girlfriend, that it would be hard to ever see her as a sister now? Would Keaton even believe him? It wasn't as if anything had really happened between them.

Maybe that was the answer. Maybe he should do for his brother what his brother had done for him back in college. If Rylee was a cheater, better that Keaton know it now than in the future when it would hurt more.

Yes, it might work. It would tear his heart out, but he'd do it for his brother. Rylee didn't deserve him.

Not tonight, though. Tonight he'd make sure his mother got to her room at the back of the house safely and then ride out to the cows in the dark. Maybe by the time he got back he could find a way out of this mess.

R ylee followed Beck's mother to her sizeable craft room, which had numerous cupboards and tables, one of which held a sewing machine.

"Thank you for letting me stay here."

"We're glad to meet you." Gracie beamed her a smile. "And I'm particularly glad you and my son are getting along so well."

Was it that obvious? Gracie had only seen her and Beck together a few minutes. She must be a sensitive woman because Rylee already felt eager to see where this thing between her and Beck would lead.

"There's a bathroom through that door," Gracie said. "Just change into the dress. Inside out, though, okay? It'll be easier to see what we need to do."

That sounded logical to Rylee, whose only experience sewing was at Lily's House where the girls were encouraged to mend their own clothes. She could sew a straight seam, replace a button, and even approximate a rough blind stitch by hand, but that was about it.

A few minutes later, she was standing in front of Gracie,

who began to pin the dress. "Tell me about yourself," she said. "Keaton only talked to Delfina when he called, and the rest of our communications about your visit have been through text. And you know how he is—not very effusive. Writing was never his strong suit."

"I work for a mortgage broker," Rylee said. "I manage a team. It's a good job. Challenging. I really like it."

"How did you meet Keaton?"

"Through my roommate. She's engaged to the man Keaton's working for." She hesitated before adding, "I bet you're looking forward to him coming back home."

"Oh, yes. It's been a long six months, but it's almost over. And I'm glad he met you."

"I'm glad I met him too." *Or I never would have met Beck,* she added silently.

The talk moved to her sister, and before Rylee could help herself, she was telling Gracie about the rehearsal dinner, seeing her mother again, and the foster homes she'd lived in. Gracie took it all in stride, asking the right questions and showing a wry sense of humor that Rylee loved.

"I think that's it," Gracie said. "Go change and bring the dress back here, okay? I think I'm ready to lie down now, but I'll tackle the seams first thing in the morning with Delfina's help."

"I really appreciate this."

Gracie laughed. "Better wait until you see it. You'll either put your sister to shame, or we'll be patching the holes I make."

"I don't think it could be too much worse." Smiling, Rylee turned to go, but Gracie's hand on her arm stopped her.

"If you need anything, please let me know. You don't know what it means to have my son find someone special."

"Thank you." Rylee escaped before the moment became weird.

Was there something wrong with Beck that his mother was this excited to have them together after only one day? She laughed the worry away. There was nothing wrong with that hunk of man.

After leaving the dress in the now-deserted craft room, Rylee wandered back into the living room, but the light was out and Beck was nowhere to be seen.

Fighting disappointment, she went up the stairs to her room, where she found her clothes from the afternoon cleaned and folded on her bed. The baby blue tennis shoes had also been washed and while they were still a bit wet, they looked nearly brand new. She'd have to thank Delfina tomorrow for working her magic.

As she readied for bed, she found a text from Tara. *Well? How's hottie? Tell me everything.*

Instead of answering, Rylee went downstairs for water. She was leaving the kitchen when Beck came in the back door. His eyes ran over her striped pink pajamas, a hint of a smile coming to his lips. Why couldn't she have remembered a robe or a least worn something more mature?

"Hi," she said a bit breathlessly. "Where'd you go?"

"To check on the cows."

"Oh, I wish I could have gone. That would be interesting."

"It's a bit of a ride." His eyes were doing funny things to her skin wherever his gaze landed—which for some reason seemed to be anywhere except her face.

"I like rides. Lily's House has a couple horses the girls take care of." She tried to catch his gaze, but his eyes still avoided hers. "Is everything okay?" she asked.

"I didn't know you knew Keaton."

Is that what this was about? "I'm sorry about that," she said. "I couldn't have known when I met you. I didn't even remember the name of the ranch until I checked Keaton's text after leaving the fair. But I guess it doesn't matter, right? We didn't need Keaton to hit it off."

"We didn't need Keaton?" In two steps he was next to her, his hands rubbing her upper arms. "You mean to do this?"

His touch was delicious, and she sighed a little with relief. His mouth came closer. This was it, the kiss that had been inevitable since the moment they met.

Closer.

And then he stopped. A groan escaped his throat. "Go to bed, Rylee. Go now. Or I won't be responsible for what I do next."

"What?"

"You heard me."

An order, not a request. Part of her wanted to retreat, the little abandoned girl part, but the part of her that was strong, the real her, glared at him, hands on her hips.

"I don't know what's going on with you, Beck. I like you a lot—or at least I did. I thought we had a great day. I thought we had a connection. But you're scaring me right now. So I am going, and not because you ordered me to, but because you're being a big jerk." She whirled and strode away from him.

"Wait, Rylee."

She heard steps coming after her, but she took the stairs two at a time and went into her bedroom, shutting and locking the door. Tomorrow, she'd get a hotel or bend her own rules and stay with her mother.

There was a tap on the door, but she ignored it, and after a while the footsteps there faded. Slipping into bed, she put the pillow over her head like she had as a child, ever since the time she'd been forced to sleep in a drafty shed alone. Back then she'd hidden to fool the monsters she was sure lurked in the corner. Now it was to hide from the sadness growing in her heart.

The bridesmaid brunch was in full swing. At first it hadn't gone badly. Marlee was bright and happy as they had their nails and hair done at a salon. Then Marlee's soon-to-be sister-in-law, her parent's credit card in hand, took them to enjoy a tasty meal in a private room at a restaurant. The matching pearl necklaces and earrings handed out to the bridesmaids in a teal clutch purse were far more than Rylee had expected as a gift.

After the meal they sat chatting, most of the girls drinking freely. Marlee directed the waiter to fill Rylee's wine glass again, but she shook her head.

"I'm driving. But you go ahead." She'd noticed that up until now the waiter had only poured juice for Marlee.

"She can't," Elena said. "Because of the baby."

"Baby?" Rylee blinked in surprise.

"Yeah. She's preggo. Didn't you know?"

"No." Rylee had assumed Marlee wasn't drinking because she didn't want to have a hangover at the wedding that afternoon.

"Shut up, Elena." Flushing a bright red, Marlee jumped

to her feet and dragged Elena away from the table. "We're going to the bathroom. We'll be right back."

Rylee sat staring awkwardly at the other three girls. They had been at the table last night with her, but she'd already forgotten their names.

"Like it's any secret why the snotty Sweeny family is even permitting this wedding," the girl closest to Rylee muttered, tucking her dark, chin-length hair behind her ear with an exaggerated sweep. "It's only because Calvin's mommy wants to get her clutches on the baby." The other girls laughed.

"They would have gotten married anyway, I'm sure," Rylee said in her sister's defense. "The baby might just have hurried things along a bit."

"Not if his mom didn't approve," the dark-haired girl retorted. "If she asked him to jump, he'd ask how high. Don't get me wrong. I love Marlee, but I think Calvin's mom is going to drive her crazy."

All the girls toasted that comment with another drink, and Rylee decided it was time to call Tara. Maybe her friend could give her some insight as to what to do about both Marlee and Beck. Marlee was evidently embarrassed about her condition, and Beck . . . she had no clue what to think about his strange behavior.

Slipping from the room without any of the remaining girls noticing, she found a relatively deserted corner of the restaurant near a hallway, which she assumed led to the kitchen. On her phone, she discovered a text from Jason, her friend from work, saying he definitely wasn't making it to the wedding. She sighed, having already expected as much.

She was halfway through a text asking if Tara had time to talk when she heard voices coming from the hallway. "It still wasn't for you to say. My baby, my body, my secret." Definitely Marlee speaking, her voice high and stressed. Rylee's hand froze on her phone.

"I thought everyone knew," Elena said. "She's your sister. Why doesn't she know?"

Marlee sighed. "Because we're not close, and she's only here because my mother insisted. She thought Rylee would make us look good with your mother, that's all. More of a typical family."

"But she's your sister."

"So? I don't even want her here. Why should I? I've tried everything I know to subtly get rid of her, but she just doesn't get it."

"You're talking about ordering the wrong size for her dress, aren't you?"

"And not letting her bring a date last night and making her pay her plus-one for the wedding dinner."

"But why on earth would you do all that? I couldn't imagine getting married without Molly around."

"My little sister isn't like yours." Marlee paused for a few heartbeats, heartbeats that seem to be torn from Rylee's chest. "She's always looked down on me," Marlee continued. "Always. Every time she'd come home, she was full of 'Don't do this' or 'I'm too good for that.' She shouldn't be here and especially not to gloat over my mistakes."

They rounded the corner, coming to an abrupt stop when they saw Rylee. Elena gasped and Marlee's nostrils flared, her eyes growing wide.

Rylee refused to cry or let herself become visibly upset. *See? They never change,* she thought.

"You know what?" she said slowly. "I only came because my big sister asked me to. I thought you wanted me. But I should have known better. She only wanted you, and you only wanted me gone. I was just something to pull out when Mom needed more government money, or someone you could make steal candy bars and cigarettes from the store. You and Mom never wanted me. Not then, not now, not ever. Goodbye, Marlee. I hope everything goes well, with your wedding and your baby."

Rylee pushed the purse with her pearl necklace into her sister's hands and walked away. She didn't cry. At least not until she was in her car. She hated herself for the tears. And she couldn't fathom how she'd managed to get herself into this position. She'd vowed not to let herself become emotionally involved, and yet here she was, upset over her family.

No, not really her family. Her family was Tara and Lily, and the others from Lily's House.

Still the tears came because having Lily and the others was wonderful, but it made her expect more with her own family.

Rylee drove without thinking about her destination until she came to a stop outside the B&K Ranch. She wasn't recovered enough to go inside yet, but when she was, she wouldn't have to do anything except toss her clothes into her suitcase and drive two hours back to Phoenix with a useless dress that she would never wear. She wouldn't even have to see Beck as he was probably working. What did she care about him anyway? He'd gone from attentive and charming in one instant to scary and intimidating the next. His mother was right to worry about him finding someone.

She climbed from the car and started walking, but she didn't go to the porch. Instead, she rounded the house and made her way past a barn and a fenced yard where chickens pecked at the ground. A smaller wire pen sat in a corner of the larger one, and inside, tiny yellow chicks huddled together in the shade of a coop, separated from the larger chickens.

She crouched next to the fence. They were too far away to touch but watching them walking about so innocently made her smile. She'd stay here until she was sure her emotions were under control, and then she'd go inside to pack.

Beck found Rylee staring at the chicks but apparently not really seeing them because he called her name three times before she finally looked at him. She wore a fluttery, flowery skirt that rippled in the wind, and a delicate off-white blouse of the same gauzy material. Her long hair was swept up in an elaborate twist, with delicate curls peeking out everywhere. She looked amazing, except her face was sad, and when she finally did look up at him, she didn't smile.

"You okay?" he asked, hunkering down next to her. He was pretty sure she'd been crying. Was it over him? He tried to stifle that hope because she wasn't his and never would be.

"Lousy day," she said.

"The brunch didn't go well?"

"Not really."

She didn't seem inclined to talk, but the sadness in her eyes ate at him. "Tell me."

"I'm not staying for the wedding after all. My sister doesn't want me here." Her smile was forced. "The too-big dress should have been my first clue."

"What about Keaton?"

She shrugged. "Why should he care?"

Beck had no answer to that. Weddings were women's domain, that was for sure, but no matter how important Keaton's work was to the ranch, he still thought his brother was an insensitive fool not to be here with the woman he loved, especially if he planned to announce his own engagement tomorrow.

Rylee arose and began walking back to the house. Beck ached to say something, but it was better this way. Because last night when he'd had his chance to prove she was a cheater, he hadn't been able to do it. He told himself it was because he couldn't hurt his brother, but if he was honest, it was really himself he was protecting.

"About last night," he began.

She shook her head. "You don't have to explain. I just need to get my things from the house. I'm going home."

"You're really not going to the wedding?"

"Nope."

"What will you tell Keaton?"

"The truth."

That surprised him. But did she mean about the two of them or the falling out she must have had with her sister?

He opened the back door and led her into the kitchen.

"About time you got here," Beck's mother said. "We've

been watching you two out the window. How are the new chicks?" She was seated at the kitchen table with a visitor who wore a peach dress and whose blond hair swept up in a mess of curls like Rylee. At the stove, Delfina was making tea.

"They look healthy," Beck mumbled. He didn't know the stranger, but the way Rylee glared told him she definitely did.

"This is Marlee, Rylee's sister," Beck's mother said.

Beck nodded. Normally he'd say it was nice to meet her, but he hated the way Rylee's hands fisted at her side. He moved closer to her. She glanced at him, and for a moment their eyes met and held. A world of emotion in that minute. He wanted to fight for her, to be her hero. But if he did, he might be nothing more than a slime ball who stabbed his brother in the back.

"What are you doing here?" Rylee said to her sister, her voice soft and calm.

"I had to talk to you, so I called Lily's House and she knew where you were staying. Look, I'm sorry." Marlee jumped up from the table. "I'm sorry for all of it. I didn't mean . . . I'm just . . ." She stopped and swallowed hard.

"Why don't we give you two a minute alone?" His mother gathered her crutches, motioning to Delfina, and the two older women left the room.

Beck folded his arms across his chest and planted his feet firmly. No way was he going anywhere, not with Rylee looking like her best friend had died. She was family, or nearly, and he wouldn't leave her alone. If Keaton wasn't man enough to be here, he'd stand up for her himself.

Rylee looked at him, her mouth opening slightly as if to

speak, then curving in a smile instead. A bit mocking, but it was better than the sadness.

Her gaze shifted back to her sister. "You didn't mean what? Not inviting me to stay with you? Ordering my dress too big? Telling me to go to the rehearsal dinner alone?"

Marlee slumped back into her seat. "His mother hates me. The only reason she's letting Calvin marry me is because of the baby, and . . . and . . . I'm jealous of you."

Rylee leaned over and slapped her open hand on the table. "Jealous of me! Are you crazy? You're the one who had Mom all your life. You're the one who had Dad when he was alive. You're the one who was wanted by both of them. They didn't give you to strangers."

"Yeah." Marlee's face scrunched as she struggled with her emotions. "Maybe. But I'm the one who had to endure their fighting. I'm the one who had to figure out how to eat when Mom was so drunk she couldn't get out of bed. I'm the one who had to steal clothes from my friends. Don't you see? I always thought you were the lucky one."

Marlee was crying, and Beck looked away from her face, easing away now that it didn't seem likely they would kill each other.

"They should have taken me away too," Marlee whispered. "But they didn't. They only cared about you. The cute little girl. You got to live with people who made dinner. You had a social worker who saw that you had clothes and cared when you got good grades. You learned. And then you had Lily's House and all those girls. I didn't have anyone. Not even you."

Rylee stared at her sister. "I didn't know. I never thought about it that way."

"I didn't want to tell you. I didn't want you to feel sorry for me. But I know that most of the problems between us are because of me. I'm the one who didn't try."

Rylee went around the table and pulled her sister into a hug. "It's okay. It's going to be okay. We can start over."

"I'd like that." Marlee wilted in her sister's arms. "Please stay. Not for Mom. For me."

Rylee didn't speak, but she nodded.

They separated and silence stole over the kitchen as Marlee dabbed at her face. "Then you'll come to the wedding?"

Rylee nodded, though Beck could swear she was still reluctant, but if asked, he'd never be able to say what tipped him off.

"Thank you." Marlee's eyes went to Beck. "Are you her date? All the bridesmaids are bringing their dates. It's paid for. Please come, both of you. And we've ended up with a few extra dinners, if you want to bring a couple more friends."

Rylee opened her mouth, and Beck knew she was going to say that he wouldn't be coming.

No way would he let her walk into that alone. "I'll be there," he said, beating her to it. "Thank you for the invitation."

Marlee nodded. "I'd better go. Mom's probably going crazy wondering where I ran off to." She dug into her ridiculously large peach-colored bag and pulled out a smaller teal purse, which she set on the table as if afraid to give it directly to Rylee. "Your pearls. Come at two for pictures. I'll see myself out." With a nod at Beck, Marlee hurried from the room.

"You didn't have to agree," Rylee said when her sister was gone. "I can go alone."

"Hey, it's a free meal, right? Besides, Keaton said I should go with you if you needed a date."

She rolled her eyes. "Great, now I'm a charity case."

He wanted to tell her he was going because he wanted to be with her, that he wanted to protect her, but with Keaton standing between them, neither admission was a good idea. "Come on. It'll be fun."

"Okay. Thank you."

A rustle at the kitchen doorway signaled his mother's return. "Did your sister leave already?" At Rylee's nod, she added, "Well, I hope you worked things out because your dress is ready to try on."

9

Rylee repaired her makeup in the bathroom upstairs and then put on the dress Gracie and Delfina had worked on all morning. She stepped into it, pulled it up, and looked into the mirror. She could only get it zipped up halfway by herself, but she could tell it was perfect. Loose enough to sit comfortably yet form-fitting enough to show off her figure. It no longer looked as if she were wearing her mother's dress. Only the neckline was a little large, and she doubted anyone would be able to tell. After the horror stories she'd heard about bridesmaid dresses, she'd expected to hate the dress, but she loved it.

She opened the purse and removed the box of pearls— and also found seventy dollars, the price she'd paid for the plus-one. Apparently, her sister was really repentant if she'd returned that. Rylee chuckled as she clasped on the necklace.

The pearls were the crowning touch to her ensemble, and Rylee let her fingers rest on them, reliving the moment when Marlee had given them to her at the bridesmaid brunch before everything had gone sideways. The wonder of having something so nice, something she would be able to look at years from now and be able to say, "My big sister gave me these." She'd never had that before. Well, she did have the miniature toy figurine, a little white dog that she'd taken home with her when her mother let her go back to foster care the first time. It had been one of Marlee's cast-offs, but she'd treasured it for no reason she could ever identify.

Shaking her head, she stepped into her shoes, packed her phone, lipstick, and a few bills into the clutch purse, and went down the stairs, wobbling a little on the unfamiliar heels. No one was in the entry, so she made her way to the family room where Gracie and Delfina sat together on the couch. At their urging, she did a twirl.

"Now that's a nice fit," Gracie said.

Delfina popped up from the couch to finish pulling up her zipper. "Nice, indeed. We did a good job."

"Thank you so much," Rylee said. "I didn't think . . . I mean, you didn't have . . ."

Gracie laughed. "Just leave it at thank you." Her eyes went beyond Rylee. "Oh, there you are, Beck. You look almost as good as Rylee."

Slowly, Rylee turned to see Beck standing behind her. Her breath caught in her throat. He looked different in the dark suit and pale green shirt, without his cowboy hat and his hair combed back. Yet it wasn't his handsomeness that stole her breath, but the way he stared at her. In a way no one had ever stared at her before. All the tension rushed from her body. Whatever weirdness had happened between them last night, maybe it would be all right.

"Thought we'd go matching," he said, indicating his shirt. "Or kind of."

"It's perfect."

"Shall we go then?" He proffered an arm. "We're cutting it short if you need to be there by two."

"Actually, that's for pictures. Why don't you meet me there later? It's going to be a long two hours before the actual ceremony."

"I'll go now. A woman as beautiful as you needs an escort," he said. To Gracie and Delfina, he added. "Don't you agree, ladies?" They nodded and chimed their agreement.

What could she say to that?

"Okay. Let's go. Thank you." As she waved goodbye to the women, she noticed a line of worry between Gracie's eyes. Before she could think too much of it. Beck swept her out of the house.

Outside at the country club where the wedding was being held, Beck watched the picture-taking. Logically, he knew the other women in the wedding party were beautiful, but it was only Rylee he saw. Whenever she wasn't needed for a picture, she sat with him in the chairs set up for the wedding. They laughed more than they probably should have, drawing attention from everyone in the wedding party. Watching her come toward him each time was like fitting the last pieces of a puzzle together. There was nowhere else either of them belonged.

When he pulled out his phone and started taking his own pictures of her, he knew it had to stop. He had to text Keaton because he'd never make it through the rest of the night without sweeping Rylee into his arms and kissing her senseless.

Keaton, you need to get here right now. He texted. *Not tomorrow. Now. I know you had a cattle drive this morning, and you probably aren't finished yet, but you need to hop in the shower, put on a suit, and get to this wedding tonight, even if you don't make it until later. Rylee needs you. Come now.*

The answer came quickly, which told Beck his brother wasn't that far from civilization. *What happened? Did her family do something? It means a lot to me to have you helping her.*

"No, *your family* is going to do something," Beck wanted to say. He texted back: *Your whole future might be at stake.*

Is it the ranch? Or Mom? You're scaring me, bro.

No, it's Rylee. Hadn't he already said that? Why was Keaton more concerned about the ranch than his future fiancée? *I mean it. I don't know if I can . . .*

Can what? Walk away?

He added "be here," and sent the text.

Then you did go with her to the wedding? Beck, you can leave the ranch every now and then. Have some fun. Rylee's great. Get to know her a little.

His brother was a complete idiot. Did he want Beck to steal her away? Keaton would never know how much Beck wanted to do exactly that. But he cared too much about both his brother and Rylee to mess where he had no business messing.

JUST COME NOW! I'll text you the address.

Beck sent the address and turned off his phone as Rylee came swaying across the grass. "The pictures are all finished. Finally." She sighed and settled on the chair next to him. "The guests will be arriving soon. Have you seen my purse?"

"Your mother gathered up all the ones on that table over

there. She was worried about something getting taken with all the waiters roaming around. I think they're in that big bag there by her husband."

Rylee laughed. "Good old Leo. I like him."

"Want to go check?"

"No, I just wanted to make sure I don't lose my phone. I'll get it after the ceremony." She scanned the chairs and the surrounding area. "This is so beautiful."

He dragged his eyes from her and looked around at the expertly-manicured lawn, the well-tended plants in the expansive beds, and the colorful blooms spilling from numerous decorative urns. A small lake was a rich backdrop to the rose and vine-covered pergola, where presumably the bride and groom would be married.

"I guess," he said. "It's a little tame."

She grinned. "I know what you mean. At Lily's House, the girls always get married in the church," Rylee said. "Then we go back to Lily's House and party or to a reception center Lily somehow arranged for a steal. We do all our own dresses, food, and flowers. By contrast, this could be something from a magazine."

"Hopefully that means the food is good."

"I *am* hungry."

He felt a little guilty at that. She was his guest and he'd been so intent on finishing his work and getting ready this afternoon that he hadn't thought to offer her lunch. "We could sneak away for a bit."

She punched him playfully. "You just want to get out of here. I told you it was going to be long and boring."

"Hey, you're in the pictures. Now you can leave anytime, and they'll never know. Just say the word."

Rylee covered her mouth, presumably to quiet her laugh. "Stop it already. You know I have to stand up there with her. Let's move closer before there's no more room."

The guests gathered quickly and soon the wedding started. Beck's right hand rested against his thigh, and he couldn't decide if it was coincidence or planned that her left hand, halfway on her own lap, touched his. But he wasn't moving away, Keaton or no Keaton.

Eventually, Rylee had to stand with the other bridesmaids and an older lady took her chair. The bride and groom exchanged vows that seemed a little rehearsed to Beck, but the passionate kiss the new couple exchanged was met with a murmur of approval.

Afterward, during cocktails, Beck and Rylee talked with her mother and stepfather. Rylee looked nothing like her mother, whose face was worn and a bit haggard, but now that he'd had time to study them, Rylee did look a bit like her sister.

"Rylee!" Marlee came toward them, her new husband in tow. "I've been wanting to tell you. That dress looks amazing on you."

Rylee's smile seemed genuine. "Beck's mother took it in a bit."

"I'm glad." The sisters hugged, and the gesture was less awkward than it had appeared at his house earlier.

As Marlee moved on to greet other guests, Beck took Rylee's hand. "Glad you came?"

"Yes. But thank you for coming with me. It would have been harder alone." She took a sip of her drink, and for a moment he was distracted by the way her tongue ran along her upper lip, sweeping away the extra liquid from her glass.

"A guy from work was coming with me, but I think his girlfriend nixed it, even though we're just friends."

Beck felt a surge of jealousy toward the unnamed friend, which was silly. "Keaton should be here instead of me."

"Are you kidding? Not with that cattle drive today. Besides, he says he hates these things."

"Don't we all?" Beck said a little more darkly than intended.

Rylee's eyebrows rose. "Oh, yeah? You could have fooled me. Poor baby."

She was right, he was enjoying himself. Too much in fact. He vowed to stop that right now. Was it possible she didn't realize she was flirting? Or maybe she didn't understand the effect it had on him. He had to believe that because she didn't seem the cheating kind. No, not at all. In fact, she seemed quite the opposite. She was here for her family, after all, and he'd seen up close how difficult that had been for her.

Cocktails gave way to a seated dinner inside the club, where the veal practically melted in his mouth. "Okay, this is really good. I'll have to see who they buy from and steal all their secrets, so my cattle taste even better."

Rylee laughed. "Look, they've set up a dance floor outside. Let's go dance."

"No."

"What, don't you dance?" Her smile mocked him.

"Yeah, I dance." *Just not with you,* he added silently.

"I don't believe it. Come on. I wrestled pigs for you. You can give me one dance."

"It was hardly wrestling." But he let her pull him to his feet. Truth was, he wanted to feel her in his arms. To hold her. What would it hurt? Just one time. It might be his only chance.

One dance turned into two, and then three and four. Her cheek was so close, her lips tantalizing. If he didn't break away, he was going to kiss her. Summoning all his resolve, he ordered himself to step away. It was that moment he spied his brother across the dance floor.

Heat rushed over Beck, but he couldn't tell if it was anger or embarrassment. How long had Keaton been watching them? Long enough, probably, to know that Beck wasn't exactly being brotherly. This was it. Now or never. He'd have to turn her over—or fight for her.

He wanted Rylee. He wanted to get to know her better, to meet her friends, to learn all her favorite foods and what made her happy. And he definitely wanted to explore her lips in detail. But he loved his brother. He couldn't have both.

"It's about time," he growled. Taking Rylee's hand, he led her from the dance floor.

"Where are we going?" she asked.

"To see Keaton. He's here."

Rylee looked confused. "Why?"

"For you, of course. Let's go."

Rylee stumbled a little as Beck pulled her through the dancers in his eagerness to get to Keaton. Why Keaton was here, she couldn't imagine. But she was annoyed. All afternoon, Beck had been acting strange—warm and flirty one minute and withdrawn and anxious the next. Almost as if he were trying not to like her, or maybe hiding something. But for the past few dances, there had been nothing between them. Nothing but laughter and their obvious attraction. She suspected his brother's appearance might ruin everything

For a moment, she'd thought he might kiss her. She'd *wanted* him to kiss her.

They'd reached Keaton, but he wasn't alone. His fiancée, Leah, was at his side, and both stared at her and Beck, questioning smiles on their faces.

"Okay, here she is," Beck said, dropping Rylee's hand like it burned him. "Safe and sound." His voice came out hoarse.

"Uh, you guys look like you're having fun," Keaton said uncertainly. "Rylee, are you okay?"

That was an odd question. "What makes you think I'm not? And what are you doing here?"

"Beck told me something was wrong, so Leah and I dropped everything and made the drive as fast as we could." Keaton took Leah's hand, smiling at her.

Beck stared down at their linked hands. "Leah?"

"Yeah, Lee, for short," Keaton said.

"I thought Rylee was Lee."

"No, she's Rylee."

Understanding washed over Rylee. "You thought I was Keaton's fiancée? All this time?"

"Well, not all . . . Wait. You're not?" Beck stared back and forth between the three of them. "But Mom said . . . Delfina thought . . ." He trailed off.

Keaton grinned. "I think there's been a little mistake."

"A big mistake." Rylee glared at Beck. "Why didn't you

just ask me?" Did he seriously think she'd be flirting the way she had with him if she was exclusively dating another man? To Keaton she added, "I'm sorry you came all the way out here, but you might as well get a drink and dance a little, if you're staying."

"Actually, if everything's okay here, I think I'll head on home to introduce Mom to Leah. She's been sending me some weird texts about my intentions toward Lee. Now I think she must have been talking about Rylee." Keaton slapped Beck on the shoulder. "You guys must have some chemistry if Mom noticed. I told you Rylee was fun. You two should go dance some more."

Rylee clenched her hands at her side and turned to watch them leave. She was furious and embarrassed, but most of all disappointed. Beck hadn't come here tonight because he wanted to be with her. He'd come because she was needy and he'd been doing his brother a favor. No wonder Beck had acted so strangely.

"Rylee!" Beck said, his voice a little too loud in her ear.

She took a breath and turned to face him. "What?"

"Just this." Beck pulled her tightly against him. His mouth came down on hers. Fervent, scorching, questioning.

For an instant, she was tempted to push him away. He'd made terrible assumptions. He'd been a jerk. But he'd also been kind and wonderful and she was crazy attracted to him. Being here in his arms was right and good and filled every wish she'd ever had about finding someone to love. Someone who was meant for her. Lily had always said that even the best relationships required a healthy dose of forgiveness.

She gave a little sigh and answered with her own fiery kiss.

People passed them in the dimming light, but they were mere blips on her radar. All that mattered was Beck and his touch. Their kissed deepened, sending a blaze of excitement coursing through her entire body. She was flying and drowning all at once. Rushing and burning. Living. They were the only people in the world who had ever shared a kiss like this.

"I've been wanting to do that ever since you fell in the mud," he whispered against her lips. "And I have to warn you, I might never stop."

That was perfectly okay with Rylee. Her hands went up around his neck. "Prove it."

And he did just that.

Rachel Branton has worked in publishing for over twenty years. She loves writing women's fiction and traveling, and she hopes to write and travel a lot more. As a mother of seven, it's not easy to find time to write, but the semi-ordered chaos gives her a constant source of writing material. She's been known to wear pajamas all day when working on a deadline, and is often distracted enough to burn dinner. (Okay, pretty much 90% of the time.) A sign on her office door reads: Danger. Enter at Your Own Risk. Writer at Work. Under the name Rachel Branton, she writes romance, romantic suspense, and women's fiction. Rachel also writes urban fantasy, paranormal romance, and science fiction under the name Teyla Branton. For more information, a free ebook, or to sign up to hear about new releases, please visit www.RachelBranton.com.